LESSONS IN DESIRE

What Reviewers Say About MJ Williamz's Work

Shots Fired

"MJ Williamz, in her first romantic thriller has done an impressive job of building up the tension and suspense. Williamz has a firm grasp of keeping the reader guessing and quickly turning the pages to get to the bottom of the mystery. *Shots Fired* clearly shows the author's ability to spin an engaging tale and is sure to be just the beginning of great things to follow as the author matures."—*Lambda Literary*

"Williamz tells her story in the voices of Kyla, Echo, and Detective Pat Silverton. She does a great job with the twists and turns of the story, along with the secondary plot. The police procedure is first rate, as are the scenes between Kyla and Echo, as they try to keep their relationship alive through the stress and mistrust."—*Just About Write*

Forbidden Passions

"*Forbidden Passions* is 192 pages of bodice ripping antebellum erotica not so gently wrapped in the moistest, muskiest pantalets of lesbian horn dog high jinks ever written. While the book is joyfully and unabashedly smut, the love story is well written and the characters are multi-dimensional. …*Forbidden Passions* is the very model of modern major erotica, but hidden within the sweet swells and trembling clefts of that erotica is a beautiful May–September romance between two wonderful and memorable characters."—*The Rainbow Reader*

Visit us at www.boldstrokesbooks.com

By the Author

Shots Fired

Forbidden Passions

Initiation by Desire

Speakeasy

Escapades

Sheltered Love

Summer Passion

Heartscapes

Love on Liberty

Love Down Under

Complications

Lessons in Desire

LESSONS IN DESIRE

by

MJ Williamz

2017

LESSONS IN DESIRE
© 2017 BY MJ WILLIAMZ. ALL RIGHTS RESERVED.

ISBN 13: 978-1-63555-019-1

THIS TRADE PAPERBACK ORIGINAL IS PUBLISHED BY
BOLD STROKES BOOKS, INC.
P.O. BOX 249
VALLEY FALLS, NY 12185

FIRST EDITION: SEPTEMBER 2017

CREDITS
EDITOR: CINDY CRESAP
PRODUCTION DESIGN: SUSAN RAMUNDO
COVER DESIGN BY SHERI (GRAPHICARTIST2020@HOTMAIL.COM)

Acknowledgments

First and foremost, I'd like to thank my wife, Laydin, whose unwavering support keeps me going. I'd also like to thank Sarah and Inger for reading this book while I was writing it and offering invaluable input.

Of course, I need to thank Rad and Sandy and Cindy, and all the folks at BSB for giving my books a home and for working so tirelessly to make me a better author.

Last, but not least, I'd like to thank you, the readers, without whom none of this would be possible.

Dedication

For Laydin, my everything

CHAPTER ONE

Crockett woke up and reached out a hand. It lighted on a soft, supple body lying next to her.

"Hey, Serena," she said. "Are you awake?"

"I could be persuaded."

Crockett grinned. "Excellent answer."

She skimmed her hand over Serena's full figure, then brought it up to rest on her breast. She had more than ample bosoms, just like Crockett liked. Crockett propped herself up on her elbow so she could watch Serena's nipple grow as she played with it. When it was nice and hard, Crockett sucked it deep into her mouth. She felt it grow harder yet and flicked her tongue over it to encourage it.

Crockett felt it poking the roof of her mouth, so gave it one more hard suck then released it to take her other one. She repeated her actions, and soon Serena was begging for more. And more was just what Crockett planned to give her.

She kissed down Serena's body until she came to where her legs met. She spread them wide and made herself comfortable. She licked the length of her before darting her tongue inside to taste her creamy center. She replaced her tongue with her fingers and moved her mouth to Serena's swollen clit. She licked and sucked on it and Serena cried out as Crockett took her to one powerful orgasm.

When Serena had had enough, Crockett moved up next to her and kissed her.

"Your turn now," Serena said. She kissed down Crockett until she had one of her breasts under her mouth. "Your breasts suit you perfectly."

"You don't think they're too small?" Crockett said.

"No. Not for you. You're long and lean, and your small breasts are perfect for your build."

Further conversation was not invited as she lowered her mouth on Crockett's nipple and sucked hard on it. Crockett drew a sharp intake of breath. Damn, that felt good. She ran her hands through Serena's long, dark hair.

"You sure know what you're doing," Crockett said.

"Mm."

"That's right. Don't stop. Oh, God, Serena, please don't stop." Crockett's nipples were directly wired to her clit, and occasionally, if her partner for the night was good enough, they could get her to climax simply by sucking on her tits. It didn't happen often, but she was so close.

Serena didn't stop. She sucked harder and ran her hand down Crockett's body. She found her clit solid and ready for her. Crockett felt her clit twitch as Serena rubbed it. She was close, so very close. She was thrashing on the bed.

"Oh yes, please, oh God, please," she said, then, "Oh, God, yes!"

She arched, frozen, as the orgasm crashed over her body.

After she collapsed back onto the bed, Crockett pulled Serena close to her. Now came the awkward time. How to get rid of Serena? Sure, they'd had fun, but it was all in fun. Still, Crockett didn't want to be a jerk.

"You want to get a cup of coffee or something?" she asked.

"Ah, thanks, but I should get going. Maybe we'll see each other around, huh?"

"Yeah. I'm sure we will."

Serena got out of bed and quickly dressed. She left and Crockett was alone in the house. With the exception of Archie, her cat, who was rubbing against her legs demanding breakfast.

She fed him then looked around for something to eat for herself. Her cupboards were pretty bare. She'd have to go shopping. But she wasn't in the mood to do that just yet. First, she made coffee, then she called her best friend, Melinda, to see if she wanted to go out for breakfast.

"Hey, Crockett," Melinda answered the phone. "What's up?"

"I'm starving. You want to go grab a bite?"

"Sure."

"I'll meet you at The Nest in fifteen?"

"I'll be there."

Crockett pulled up just as Melinda was getting out of her car. She waited for Crockett to park her truck and they walked in together.

"Last night was so much fun," Melinda said. "We so need to do that again."

"No kidding. I love the women's bar in the summer. It's so much less crowded than when all the students are in town."

"Me, too, which makes me feel guilty since we make our living off those students."

"And they'll all be back soon enough."

"Yes, they will."

"We've only got a few weeks left of summer session. Then they're back."

"Oh, well. So, did you and Serena enjoy yourselves last night?" Melinda asked.

"That we did. I was even a gentlebutch and invited her out for coffee this morning, but she declined."

"Wow. That was decent of you. So, any plans to see her again?"

"Nope. She gave me the ol' 'maybe I'll see you around' bit."

"Well, I'm sure that didn't break your heart," Melinda said. "You're not really the second date type."

"No, I'm not."

"Do you think you're ever going to settle down?"

"Sure, why not? When I'm a little older and ready."

"Older? You're thirty-three. How much older do you need to be?"

"What's with the twenty questions?" Crockett said.

"I just don't see what you're so afraid of."

"I don't want to get involved because I don't want a messy break up. You can't blame me. Besides I don't see you settling down."

"That's only because I haven't found Ms. Right yet. But I'm looking."

"And I'm not. It's that simple."

They finished their breakfast and walked out to the parking lot.

"Hey," Melinda said. "We should go tubing."

"Seriously? The river will be crowded today. It's over ninety degrees already."

"Oh, come on. It'll be fun."

Crockett thought about it.

"I don't know."

"Ah, you know you want to. Hot women in bikinis tubing down the river? Lots of eye candy. You can't resist it. It's in your blood."

Crockett laughed.

"Well, when you put it that way…"

"Great. Come by my place in a half hour. I'll be ready. I'll even have beer."

"Fantastic. I'll see you then."

Crockett went home and changed into board shorts and a muscle shirt. She found her beach towel and put it in a back-pack. She also threw in some sunscreen. She was ready to go. She drove over to Melinda's place. Melinda was waiting and looked great in her shorts and bikini top. Not great like she'd ever hit on her. No, they'd been friends for too long for that. But she could still appreciate their differences. Melinda was average height and somewhat curvy, but toned, and her red hair hung to her shoulders. Yeah, she was attractive, and Crockett wondered if she'd still be with her when Crockett got off the river or if someone would snatch her up.

They drove together to the washout where their trip would end. They left Crockett's truck there and drove to Scotty's to pick up their tubes. Then they drove to the other side of the Gianella Bridge where they would start their tubing. They set their ice chest in one small tube and then lay in their individual larger tubes and pushed off to the center of the cold, slow-moving river.

Crockett kept the ice chest with her.

"Can you toss me a beer?" Melinda said.

"Better yet, I'll hand it to you."

Crockett floated over against Melinda's tube and took two beers out of the chest. She handed one to Melinda and opened one herself. She took a long pull off it. The cool liquid felt good on such a hot day.

"This was a great idea," Crockett said.

"Right?"

They floated in silence for a bit while Crockett took in the sights around her. There were scantily clad women in all shapes and sizes floating down the Sacramento.

"Are you enjoying the scenery?" Melinda finally said.

"Of course, aren't you?"

"Doesn't it scare you that some of these kids could be in our classes next year?"

"Are you kidding? I'm worried about seeing some of them that have already taken classes from us. But what the hell? We're human, right?"

"Right."

The trip passed quickly, and soon they were floating to the shore at the washout to get in Crockett's truck.

"That was fun," Crockett said. She opened the door to her truck and handed Melinda a towel.

Once they were dry, they drove up to return their tubes and to retrieve Melinda's car.

"So," Crockett said. "You want to go to The Montrose again tonight?"

"Two nights in a row? They'll think we're regulars."

"Yeah, but I'm ready to get my groove on again."

"Okay. I'll pick you up at nine?"

"Why not pick me up at seven and I'll buy dinner?"

"No kidding? I'm all over that."

"Excellent," Crockett said.

"Okay, I'll see you then."

Crockett was primed for a night at the women's bar. All those bikini clad coeds on the river had her juices flowing. She needed to find someone to take home with her that night to help alleviate some of the sexual tension. She knew Melinda thought she was too much of a player, but she couldn't help it. She enjoyed women and didn't apologize for it.

She took a shower and dressed in some khaki cargo shorts and a purple golf shirt. She wasn't conceited by any stretch, but she knew she looked good in that outfit. She always got lots of compliments when she wore it. And it hadn't failed her yet at The Montrose.

Crockett needed something to do to keep herself occupied so she did her grocery shopping, put everything away, and checked the time. It was only five. Damn. She grabbed a beer and sat in front of the television. She found a baseball game and got so into it, she started when Melinda walked in.

"Jesus, you scared me," Crockett said.

"Sorry. Is the game that good?" She motioned to the television.

"Yeah. Extra innings."

"You want to stay and watch it?"

"No. I'm good to go," Crockett said. She switched off the game and stood.

They went out for pizza and beer. They were both relaxed and ready to hit the bar by nine.

"So, you think you'll get lucky tonight?" Crockett teased her.

"If I meet Ms. Right. Or someone who looks like her," she laughed.

"I wish you'd loosen up a little bit. You might have more fun."

"You're loose enough for both of us, believe me."

Crockett laughed. It was true and she couldn't deny it.

They pulled into the parking lot. It was pretty empty, but they could already hear the music thumping from within.

"Oh, yeah," Crockett said. "This is going to be so much fun."

"I don't know how long I'll last. That time in the sun gave me quite a burn and took a lot out of me," Melinda said.

"No worries. I'll do my best to find a ride home." She winked.

"I'm sure you will."

They entered the place and made their way to the bar. Crockett ordered a beer for herself and a glass of wine for Melinda. They found a table just off the dance floor and sat there waiting for the place to fill up.

"This music is excellent," Melinda said.

"It really is. You want to dance?"

"Sure."

They got out and moved on the floor. It wasn't unusual for them to dance a few dances before the place got jumping. They both liked to dance, but once the place filled up, neither of them wanted to appear attached, so they stopped.

The place was getting full. Crockett checked her watch. It was after ten. Time to start prowling. She looked around the room and her gaze lighted on a brunette across the floor. She was full-figured and cute as a bug. She looked to be in her late twenties. Crockett approached her. She saw her dark eyes glimmer.

"Hi. Would you like to dance?" Crockett said.

"Sure."

Crockett took her hand and led her to the center of the floor. Her hand was soft and warm. They started to move to the music and Crockett was duly impressed. She danced like she was made for it.

The song ended and Crockett introduced herself above the next song.

"I'm Crockett," she said.

"Gabby."

"Nice to meet you."

"Nice to meet you, too."

They danced for another three songs when Gabby pleaded thirst.

"Can I buy you a drink?" Crockett asked as she guided Gabby to the table she and Melinda had.

"Sure. I'd like a gin and tonic, please."

"Coming right up."

Crockett looked around for Melinda and saw her on the dance floor with an older butch woman. She looked like she was having fun. Crockett shot her a thumbs-up and raised her eyebrows at her. Melinda just smiled back.

Back from the bar, Crockett handed Gabby her drink and took a long swallow of her beer. Dancing made her thirsty as well.

"You're a good dancer," Crockett said.

Gabby blushed.

"Thanks. So are you."

"Thanks. So, how come I haven't seen you around here before?"

"I'm in town visiting friends for the weekend."

Crockett's heart sank. That wasn't good for her chances of bedding the cute woman.

"Oh. Well, I don't mean to keep you from your friends. Should you be with them?"

"I'm a grown woman. And I think they'll be fine without me."

"Okay. That's good to hear."

"It is, huh?" Gabby smiled.

"Sure. I like you, Gabby."

"I like you, too, Crockett."

They danced to a few more songs and a slow song came on. Crockett opened her arms and Gabby stepped into them. She felt so right in Crockett's arms. Crockett loved the feel of her soft body pressed into her own. She wanted to get out of the bar. And fast.

When the song ended, Crockett leaned in and whispered in her ear.

"You want to get out of here?"

"Sure."

"Do you have a car here?"

"I do."

"Great. Let's go."

Crockett searched the floor again for Melinda. She waited until Melinda saw her and she waved good-bye. Melinda waved back. It was all good. The night with Gabby was just about to get fun.

Crockett gave Gabby directions to her house on the west side of town. It was a simple, ranch style house. Nothing fancy, but it was hers. She opened the door and let Gabby in first. She admired the view as Gabby's hips swayed. When Crockett closed the door, she offered Gabby a drink.

"No, thanks. I think I've had enough," Gabby said.

"Okay." Crockett was unsure what to do. She wanted to take Gabby right then, but wasn't sure if she was ready. She needn't have worried as Gabby walked into her arms. She snaked her arms around Crockett's neck and pressed against her. She kissed her lightly on the mouth.

"I've been wanting to do that all night," Gabby said.

"So have I."

Crockett held her tight and kissed her this time. It was an urgent kiss, which begged for more. She ran her tongue over Gabby's lips and begged for entrance. Gabby obliged, and soon Crockett had her tongue moving around inside Gabby's mouth. She was warm and moist and tasted vaguely of gin. Crockett couldn't wait to taste the rest of her.

"We should take this down the hall," Crockett said when the kiss finally ended. Every nerve ending was on alert. She needed Gabby in a big way.

"Yeah, we should."

Crockett took Gabby's hand and led her to her bedroom. She lit some candles and then turned to Gabby, who was sitting on the bed.

"Come here." She reached her hands out to her. "Stand up so I can undress you."

Gabby stood and Crockett could see that she was shaking. Was that a good thing? Either she was excited or nervous.

"Are you nervous?" Crockett asked.

"Not at all."

"Good."

Crockett kissed her as she reached around her to unzip the dress she was wearing. The zipper came down easily, and Crockett stepped away to watch it fall to the floor. Gabby stepped out of it. She stood there in her bra and underwear and Crockett's mouth watered. She felt moisture pool in her boxers. Gabby was beautiful.

She kissed her again and unhooked her bra, allowing her ample breasts to fall free. Crockett caught them in her hands and kneaded them lovingly. She bent to kiss the tops of them. But she wanted, needed, craved more. She knelt and pulled Gabby's panties off. She rested her cheek against Gabby's inner thigh. She was close. So close to heaven.

Crockett stood and quickly took off her own clothes. When they were both naked, she pulled Gabby in for another embrace, reveling in the feel of flesh on flesh.

"Let's lie down," Crockett said.

They climbed into her king-sized bed and lay together. Crockett propped herself up on an elbow so she could gaze at the beauty of Gabby's body. She skimmed her hand over it until she rested her hand between Gabby's legs. She was wet and warm and ready for Crockett. Crockett ran her hand over the length of Gabby, leaving no spot untouched. She dipped her fingers inside and stroked her. Then she withdrew her fingers and rubbed Gabby's swollen clit. She rubbed it hard and fast and Gabby was soon writhing on the bed. Crockett lowered her mouth and took one of Gabby's nipples in. She sucked hard as she continued to rub, and in no time Gabby cried out as the orgasm washed over her.

Gabby recovered quickly and kissed Crockett hard on the mouth. She wasted no time finding Crockett's center with her fingers and she moved them in and out until Crockett was gasping for air and begging for release. Gabby moved down her body and sucked Crockett's clit in her mouth. She ran her talented tongue over it, and Crockett pressed Gabby into her as she came.

Chapter Two

M onday morning found Crockett at the university. It was office hour time for her and she was in her office grading papers when Melinda came in.

"Professor Devine," Melinda said. "I hope I'm not interrupting."

Crockett looked up.

"Not at all, Professor O'Reilly. To what do I owe this pleasure?"

Melinda closed the door.

"I think I'm in love," Melinda almost squealed.

"What? When did this happen?"

"Her name is Terry Smith, and oh, my God, is she ever wonderful."

"Was that the woman I saw you dancing with the other night?"

"The very one."

"So, I take it things went well that night?" Crockett said.

"And yesterday and last night."

"Wow." Crockett was surprised. Melinda rarely hooked up with anyone. Sure, she'd kiss a little, but seldom went home with them. She must really like this Terry woman. "That's great."

"Yeah. Sorry I didn't call to see how your night had gone yesterday, but I was busy." She blushed.

"Totally understandable. So, are you in any shape to teach today?"

"Oh, yeah. I'm a little distracted, but I'm a professional, Crockett. It's Monday and I'm here to do my job."

"I figured."

"Speaking of which…" Melinda checked her watch. "I'd better get back to my classroom. I just had to touch base with you. I'm so excited."

She practically squealed again as she turned to leave Crockett's office. Crockett stared after her. She was happy Melinda seemed to have found someone. She wondered if she'd ever be that happy with another person. She shrugged. It wasn't that big of a deal. If she did, she did. No worries. And no hurry. She liked her life as it was now. And she wasn't a big fan of change.

Office hours ended and it was time for Crockett to teach. She stepped into her classroom and saw her small class in their seats and ready to discuss mythology. It was one of Crockett's favorite classes to teach, and her small summer session class was doing a great job keeping up with their assignments.

She taught Freshman English after that for the students who hadn't done well in the class during the regular semester. These were younger students than her first class, and they didn't do as well with their papers. But still, she taught for all she was worth and tried to teach them basic sentence structure and such.

Her final class of the day was creative writing. When it was over she had more office hours and then she got to go home. Her home was nice and quiet and she and Archie had dinner and watched a game on television.

The rest of the week passed uneventfully. More classes, more grading papers. She didn't see Melinda again until Thursday afternoon. Classes in summer session were Monday through Thursday. Crockett was just finishing up her office hours when Melinda came in.

"Hey, Professor O'Reilly. What's up?"

Melinda closed Crockett's door.

"Terry really wants to meet you," Melinda said.

Crockett raised an eyebrow.

"She does?"

"Of course. You're my best friend, Crockett."

"Okay. So, shall we all go to The Montrose tomorrow night?"

"Sure. And maybe to dinner beforehand?"

"Sounds good, but I don't know what kind of an impression I'll make on her at The Montrose. Because you know I'm going to be on the prowl."

"We'd expect nothing less." Melinda laughed. "That's why I suggested dinner before. We can chat and she can get to know you a little before you take up your position as head prowler at the club."

"Sounds like an excellent idea."

"Great. We'll pick you up at seven thirty for dinner, then?"

"Right on."

Melinda let herself out of Crockett's small office. Crockett wondered what she was getting herself into. Still, if this Terry woman was important to Melinda, she was important to Crockett. And Crockett should check her out anyway. She wanted to make sure Melinda wasn't going to get hurt.

❖

Gina Moreno went over her papers again. She was all set. She'd been accepted to the graduate English program at Chico State. She was so excited she could hardly stand it. She stared at all the boxes strewn over her apartment. She needed to unpack and settle in, but she was hot. It was hot in Chico in the summer. She opted instead to go to the pool for a while.

It was quiet by the pool, which she expected, as it wasn't a college apartment complex. So most of the residents would be at work on a Friday afternoon. There were a few people there, but not many. She dove into the water. It was cool and felt good against the heat of the day. She got out of the water and lay on a lounge chair.

"You're new here, aren't you?" a voice said.

She opened her eyes and saw a middle-aged man standing over her.

"Yes," she said. "I just moved in."

"Yeah. I'd remember if I'd seen you around. I'm David."

"Gina," she said.

"Are you new to town, Gina?" David asked.

"Yes. I just moved here from Illinois."

"Would you like me to show you around sometime?"

Oh, my God. He was hitting on her. It wasn't the first time some confused man had made moves on her, but it still made her nauseous every time.

"Thanks, but I have some friends in town that will be showing me around."

"Okay. Well, if you need anything, I'm in apartment one twenty-seven."

"Thank you," she said again, then closed her eyes and left him to go away.

She took a couple more dips in the pool and lay out for close to three hours. She was tired when she finally went back to her apartment. She stripped out of her suit and took a quick shower, then lay down for a nap. When she awoke, it was evening and she was hungry. She searched online for a nice place to eat and decided on a restaurant that sounded good. It was a creperie, and it appeared to have an incredible selection. She didn't know anyone in town except her advisor. She was a nice woman, and Gina had the feeling she was family. Not wanting to eat alone, she called Brenda and asked her to join her.

"I'd love that," Brenda said.

"Great. It'll be my treat for all you've done for me."

"That's not necessary."

"Please. I insist."

"Fine. If you insist. I'll meet you there in fifteen minutes?"

"I'll be there."

Gina pulled into the parking lot and realized she no idea what kind of car Brenda drove, which meant she had no idea if Brenda was there or not. She didn't worry about it. She walked into the restaurant to find that Brenda wasn't there yet. Gina looked around from her seat in the waiting area. Her gaze lighted on a table with three women sitting at it. Two were on one side of the table. One was a redhead and the other an older woman with silver hair. But it was the third woman who caught Gina's eye. She had cropped blond hair and eyes that sparkled. Gina couldn't tell their color from the distance, but she was drawn to her. Her insides melted. She felt an immediate and visceral response to her.

"Am I late?" Brenda asked, bringing Gina back to reality and causing her to jump.

"Are you okay?"

"Yes. Sorry. I was just lost in thought and didn't notice you come in."

"Well, I'm here." Brenda smiled. Brenda was probably forty something with dark hair pulled back into a braid she wore down her back. She was like an old hippie, only not that old, Gina thought. And she had kind green eyes.

They were shown to a table which, as luck would have it, was just across the room from the gorgeous blonde. And she was facing her. Luckily, the woman seemed too involved with the conversation at the table to notice Gina drooling over her. Gina forced her attention away from her and on to Brenda.

"Thank you for agreeing to meet me for dinner."

"No problem. I didn't have plans and this is my favorite restaurant. Plus, I know it must be hard being new to town. You'll meet people soon, but for now, you must feel like a fish out of water."

"I do. Although I did have a nice man offer to show me around today."

"Oh, really? And what did you say?"

"Let's just say he wasn't really my type."

"No? And what is your type?"

"Um, well…" Gina wasn't sure what to say. She'd heard Chico State was a fairly liberal college, but the town surrounding it was very conservative. She didn't know if she should come out to Brenda or not. She decided, what the heck? "I more prefer women."

"Ah. Well, then he most certainly wasn't your type then, was he?" She laughed. "I wondered about you. Don't worry. I'm a lesbian, too, so no judgment from me."

"Oh, that's a relief," Gina said.

The waitress came and took their orders. After she'd walked off, Brenda spoke again.

"Say, there's a women's club in town. Would you like to go there after dinner? Just to kind of check it out?"

Gina's stomach knotted. Was Brenda asking her out? She'd only invited her to dinner because she didn't know anybody else and Brenda had been very helpful to her. But she wasn't sure how to respond.

"Oh, my God. You look like you've seen a ghost," Brenda said. "I realize how that must have sounded. You probably thought you'd been hit on twice in one day. No. I just meant so you can see where it is and maybe meet some people. It wouldn't be a date."

Gina sighed in relief.

"Sure, then. That sounds great. I used to go to the women's club back home all the time. I loved the synergy there."

"I haven't been to The Montrose in a while, but the last time I was there, there were a good mix of people. The music was great and it was a lot of fun."

"Sounds good. Let's do it."

As their dinners were being served, Gina watched as the three women at the table she'd been watching stood. The blonde was tall and lean. Gina's palms almost itched to touch her. What was wrong with her? She didn't even know the woman. She turned her attention back to Brenda after watching the women walk off and enjoying the trim outline of the blonde's ass in her cargo shorts.

Gina and Brenda finished their dinners and walked out to the parking lot. It was still in the eighties outside, but at least it was a relief from the hundred degrees earlier.

"So, you want to follow me or ride with me?" Brenda said.

"I'll follow you. I have to admit, I'm really full from dinner so I don't know how late I'll want to stay, but I'll do my best to party down. Isn't that what Chico is all about?"

Brenda half smiled, half grimaced.

"That is our reputation, I'm afraid, but we do like having serious students like yourself here, too."

"Thank you."

Gina was nervous as she followed Brenda to the club. How was she supposed to act around her? Gina loved to dance. And if someone asked her to dance, she planned on doing just that. Would Brenda be out dancing, too? Or would she expect Gina to sit by her side?

They arrived at the concrete building and parked near each other in the lot. Gina could hear the thumping of music even in the parking lot. She smiled. This really could be fun.

As they walked toward the door, Gina asked, "So do you like to dance?"

"I love to dance."

"Great. So, we'll probably both be out there tearing up the dance floor, huh?"

"That's what I'm imagining."

They walked inside. There was an elevated area immediately on the left with pool tables. The bar ran along the far left wall. To the right was an elevated area with seating and there were several high tables placed along the dance floor. The tables along the dance floor were full, so Brenda and Gina walked up to the elevated area and found a table there.

"I'll buy the first round," Brenda said and headed off to the bar.

Gina settled in to watch the people as they danced and milled around. Her breath caught when she saw the three women from the restaurant sitting at a high table down on the floor. She watched the blonde scan the crowd. Her gaze went right past Gina. She didn't even stop to look at her. What was up with that? Gina wasn't conceited by any stretch, but she did know she was an attractive woman. Clearly, the blonde simply hadn't seen her.

Brenda was back at the table with their drinks.

"See anyone you'd like to dance with?"

"Oh, I'm not picky. I just love to dance. So there are plenty of potential partners here."

"Good. So, how do you work? Do you usually wait for someone to ask you or do you ask someone?"

"Depends on my mood," Gina said.

Just then a handsome woman with short dark hair interrupted them.

"Would you like to dance?" she asked Gina.

"Sure."

They cut through the crowd to the center of the floor. Gina at once felt the music move through her. She watched her partner move to the music, but soon closed her eyes and just danced. She raised her arms over her head and danced around, lost in the song. When it ended, she thanked the woman.

"How about another one?" the woman asked.

"Sure. Why not?"

They danced several more songs, and the woman escorted Gina back to her table. She noticed that Brenda was gone and looked around to find her on the dance floor.

"I'm Donna," the woman Gina had been dancing with said.

"I'm Gina."

"Nice to meet you, Gina. Can I buy you a drink?"

"Sure. I'd love a chocolate martini."

"Coming right up."

Gina relaxed while she waited for her drink. She scanned the crowd on the floor and found the blonde she'd been lusting over like a schoolgirl all night. She was out there dancing. And she knew how to dance. Gina stared at her and was startled when Donna was back with their drinks. At the same time, Brenda walked up.

"Oh," Donna said. "Are you two together?"

They both laughed.

"No," Gina said. "Nothing like that."

"Good. How's your martini?"

"It's really good."

"I'm glad."

Donna looked at Brenda.

"Can I buy you a drink?"

"Sure. I'd love a lemon drop."

"You got it."

Brenda laughed when Donna was out of earshot.

"She seems like she'd do anything to get you in bed. Even buy your friend a drink."

"Let her," Gina said.

Donna was back with Brenda's drink.

"So, what do you ladies do?" Donna asked.

"I work at the university," Brenda said.

"And I'm a grad student, just waiting for fall semester to start. And what do you do, Donna?"

"I work construction. Specifically, I pour concrete."

"That sounds like a hard job," Gina said. "Especially in the heat here."

"We get most of our work done before the afternoon heat hits."

"That's good to know."

Gina and Donna kept talking. Gina tried to engage Brenda in the conversation, but wasn't having much luck.

"I hate to break up the party," Brenda said. "But I'm wiped out. I need to head home. Gina, you can get home from here?"

"No problem. I have my trusty GPS."

"Good. Good night, you two."

"Good night, Brenda."

Gina was attracted to the compact Donna, and she was enjoying talking to her, but her gaze kept seeking out the blonde. The woman had danced with several different women throughout the night, but seemed to have settled on one. Her friends had left, but she seemed comfortable on her own.

"So what's your major?" Donna was saying.

"Hm? Oh, English."

"And what are you going to do with you master's?"

"I don't know. Teach, I hope. Preferably at a university."

"Nice. That would be a cool job."

Their conversation died for a bit. Donna cleared her throat.

"So, Gina, I don't suppose you'd like to get out of here?"

Gina contemplated her options. She wasn't the one-night stand kind of girl. But she was horny that night. The blond woman had her all worked up. And Donna was nice. And cute. And had a great body.

"Sure. We can go back to my apartment."

"Great. Let's go."

"You'll have to bear with me, though. I'll be relying on my GPS as I don't know my way around very well."

Donna laughed.

"No problem. Or you can tell me which apartments you live in and I can probably lead the way."

"Oh, good call. Let's do that."

She told her the name of the apartments.

"Sure I know where those are," Donna said. "I helped build them. Follow me."

Gina got in her car and followed Donna. She was excited. She hadn't been with a woman in a while, and while she didn't like to use or be used, she figured they were both after the same thing so there was no harm in spending the night together.

They arrived at her complex. Donna idled next to the entrance to let Gina go inside and lead her to her actual apartment. Gina parked in her spot and got out and waited as Donna found a visitor's spot.

They walked in together and, once inside, Gina offered Donna a drink.

"I'd love a beer," Donna said.

Gina went to her refrigerator and took out the last two beers. She was lucky she even had that in there. She handed one to Donna, and then sat next to her on the couch.

"Pardon the boxes," Gina said. "I haven't gotten around to unpacking."

"No wonder I'd never seen you before. You're brand new to town, aren't you?"

"I am."

Donna put her arm around Gina and they drank their beers.

"Well, if you need someone to show you around..."

"Thanks. I may take you up on that."

They finished their beers and Donna pulled Gina close. Gina felt her heart clench as Donna's lips got closer. It almost leaped out of her chest when their lips met. It had been a long time since she'd reacted that way to a kiss. She wondered how the mysterious blonde kissed, then pushed the thought out of her mind and focused on Donna.

Gina opened her mouth and welcomed Donna's tongue. Their tongues danced together briefly before Gina came up for air. She needed Donna and didn't want to wait any longer.

"Let's go to bed," she said.

"Gladly."

They made their way down the hall, past more boxes and finally ended up in the master bedroom. Gina hadn't unpacked in there yet, either, but she hoped Donna wouldn't notice anything but the bed.

They hurriedly undressed each other and fell into bed, lips and limbs moving over each other. Donna finally had Gina on her back with her legs spread wide. She climbed between them and Gina braced herself for the pleasure she was sure to come. She could feel Donna's warm breath on her and could feel herself swell in anticipation.

And then she felt Donna's tongue on her. It was an amazing sensation. She lost herself in it. Soon she could feel a ball of pressure in her center. All her energy was located there. She thought of nothing except the pleasure Donna was providing. And then the ball broke loose, shooting the wave of an orgasm throughout her body.

Chapter Three

G ina woke in the morning to an empty bed. She wasn't upset, though. She hadn't planned on anything long term with Donna. But then, she smelled coffee. Had Donna made coffee? She wrapped a bathrobe around her and padded out to the kitchen.

"Morning, gorgeous," Donna said and kissed Gina on the nose. "How'd you sleep?"

"I slept great. I can't believe you made coffee." She wasn't comfortable with how at ease Donna seemed in her house.

"I was going to make breakfast, but clearly, you haven't found the grocery store yet."

"I know. I need to shop."

"Well, how about if we shower and then I take you out for breakfast?"

"Really, that's not necessary."

"Maybe not, but it's something I'd like to do."

Gina was worried. She didn't want a relationship. Donna was nice enough, and great in bed, but she wasn't interested in her. Now, she'd have to let her down as gently as she could. She hated mornings after, which is why she seldom did one-night stands.

"Look, Donna…"

"Sh. No talking. Here. Have some coffee, then we talk."

Gina poured herself a cup of coffee and sat at the small kitchen table. Donna joined her.

"Donna, I appreciate what you're doing. I like you. I think you're a great person, but I'm really not interested in a relationship."

"Relationship? Honey, you just moved to town. How could you possibly be ready for anything like that? I had a good time with you and, sure, I'd like to see you again sometime, but I'm not looking for anything long term, either. That's not my style."

"Are you sure? Because you're not acting like that."

"Why? 'Cause I got up and made coffee? Or because I'm offering to take a friend, who has no food in her fridge, out to breakfast?"

Gina searched Donna's eyes and decided to believe her.

"Okay. Sorry, I just didn't want to have to hurt you."

"You won't. Well, you will if you don't let me shower with you this mornin'." She winked.

"I'm sure that can be arranged."

They made their way through the master bedroom to the bathroom. The shower wasn't large, but they still easily fit. Gina leaned against the wall while Donna knelt in front of her and again took her to a powerful climax. When she could trust her legs again, they washed off and went to breakfast.

Crockett woke up to find Sheri, the woman she'd taken home the previous night, still sleeping soundly. She hated to disturb her, but wanted her in the worst way. She was curvaceous and delightful and delicious. All things Crockett looked for in a bedmate. Only, she wasn't awake. Crockett contemplated waking her, but decided to get up and make coffee instead. Then, when Sheri was awake, she'd take her again.

She made the coffee and decided to bring a cup to Sheri. She had no idea how she liked her coffee, so brought it the way she drank it, with a little chocolate milk in it. When she walked in, Sheri was awake.

"I wondered where you'd disappeared to."

Sheri sat with the sheet pulled up under her chin. Too bad. Crockett wanted to see her in all her glory again. She could feel herself swelling with need. She handed a cup of coffee to Sheri.

"I didn't know how you take it."

Sheri took a sip.

"This is really good."

"Good. It's how I take mine."

She stood there watching Sheri take another sip, and then reached out and touched the top of the sheet.

"May I?" Crockett said.

Sheri blushed.

"Why?"

"Because I want to see you. I love your body and I want you so desperately right now."

"You do?"

"I do."

Crockett gave a little tug and the sheet fell down, exposing Sheri's large breasts and belly.

"Damn, you're beautiful," she said.

"Thanks. I've always been a little self-conscious about my body."

"You shouldn't be. It's amazing."

"Thank you."

Crockett took Sheri's coffee cup away from her and placed it on the dresser with her own. She climbed into bed and kissed Sheri on the mouth. She moved lower so she could suck and knead her ample breasts. She suckled Sheri until she couldn't wait any longer. She kissed down her belly to where her legs met. She sucked Sheri's clit until Sheri cried out.

And then it was her turn. She was about to explode from need and she'd learned the previous night that Sheri was very skilled at pleasing a woman. She moved her hand to Crockett's clit and softly stroked it. Crockett arched off the bed, begging for more.

Sheri moved her hand lower and entered Crockett. Crockett moaned in appreciation. Sheri was so deep and felt so good, but

Crockett needed more. She reached between her own legs and rubbed her clit while Sheri fucked her and together they took her to an earth-shattering climax.

When she'd caught her breath and had come to her senses, Crockett knew it was time for the awkward good-bye moment.

"Did you want some more coffee?" she said.

"No. I should get going."

"Are you sure?"

"Yeah. I'm sure. Thanks for last night. It was fun."

"Yeah it was."

Sheri got dressed, kissed Crockett, and saw herself out.

Crockett poured another cup of coffee and sat down to ponder what to do with her day. She was starving, so called Melinda to see about breakfast.

"Hello?" Melinda answered the phone.

"Hey. What are you and Terry up to?" Crockett said.

"Nothing. Why?"

"I wondered if you wanted to go get breakfast."

"Hold on. Let me ask Terry."

Crockett waited until Melinda came back.

"Sure. We're up for it. Give us about an hour?"

"Yeah. That'll give me time to take a shower and have some more coffee."

"Sounds good. We'll meet you at Italian Cottage?"

"That sounds great."

Crockett tossed her phone on the table and drank some more coffee. She got up, took a shower and put on some cargo shorts and an old Tubes T-shirt. She got in her truck and drove to the restaurant. She went in and saw Melinda and Terry.

"Hey, you two," she said.

"Hey," Melinda said. "Did you have fun last night?"

"I did. Did you?"

"We did. I really enjoy The Montrose. I don't know why I never went that often," Terry said.

"I'm just glad you went last weekend," Melinda said.

Crockett just looked at them. She was happy for Melinda but thought she could do without the sappy stuff. She wondered what Terry thought of her for taking a woman home with her. Not that she could judge. She took Melinda home the last weekend. But look at them now.

"What happened to the cutie you took home with you?" Terry asked.

"She beat a quick escape after coffee this morning."

"Ah. Well, from what I've heard, you were probably okay with that."

"Yeah. I'm not looking to settle down just yet."

"Then there's no reason for you to try," Terry said. "Someday, when you least expect it, she'll wander into your life."

"We'll see about that," Crockett said.

They ate their breakfast and it was time to go.

"So, I don't suppose I could convince you two to go out again tonight?" Crockett said.

"No," Terry said. "We've got plans. Sorry."

"No problem. Just thought I'd check."

Crockett said her good-byes and drove home. She was restless. She had some papers to grade, so she worked on those for a while. She played with Archie and watched some television.

She made herself some dinner and watched more television, but she was bored. She wanted to get her groove on again. She needed the warmth of another woman in her arms. She dressed and headed to the club. It was just after nine and there were plenty of spots in the parking lot, but she could still feel the asphalt thumping to the beat of the music coming from within. She walked in and found an empty bar stool. She ordered a beer and watched the game until the place got more crowded. Then it was fun time.

She turned on her stool and surveyed the women in the club. There were lots of them. A few she knew, a lot she didn't. They were all beautiful to her, but she did have her type. She liked a woman with some meat on her. She watched the women on the floor moving to the music and knew she needed to join them. She located a woman with a group of others and approached her.

"Excuse me," she said to the strawberry blonde. "Would you like to dance?"

"Sure."

Crockett took her hand and led her to the floor. It was crowded, but they found a spot on the outside edge and began to dance. The woman moved with grace and elegance. Crockett stopped at one point just to watch her move. She started to dance with her again, dancing close to her so she could brush up against her. She was soft and Crockett thought she was beautiful.

When the music died down, Crockett offered to buy her a drink.

"Sure. I'd love a glass of white wine," the woman said.

"I'll be right back."

She was back in a few minutes with a beer and a glass of white wine for her adorable dance partner.

"I'm Crockett, by the way," she said.

"Genevieve."

"That's an old-fashioned name. I like it. It suits you."

Genevieve blushed.

"Thanks. And Crockett suits you."

"Thanks."

The music grew loud again, so there was really no point in further conversation.

"You want to dance again?" Crockett called over the music.

Genevieve nodded and allowed Crockett to take her hand once again and lead her to the dance floor. They moved and grooved to several songs, and finally a slow song came on. Genevieve didn't hesitate to move into Crockett's arms. Crockett held her close and they moved as one to the song. When the song was over, Crockett ached to have Genevieve. She whispered in her ear.

"Would you like to come home with me?"

Genevieve looked shocked at first and Crockett thought for sure she'd blown it.

"Are you serious?" Genevieve said. "You want to take *me* home?"

"I am serious. What do you say?"

"Oh, my God. Well, I guess I say yes."

"You guess?" She wasn't doing much for Crockett's ego.

"I'm just so shocked. But I'd love to go home with you."

"Great."

Genevieve went over to tell her friends good-bye and walked hand-in-hand to the parking lot with Crockett. She was grinning ear to ear, which attracted Crockett to her even more.

"So, do you have a car?" Crockett asked.

"No, I rode with my friends."

"No worries. We can take my truck."

She helped Genevieve into the truck, then climbed in herself.

"You sure about this?" Crockett asked.

"Totally."

"Great."

Crockett stared at Genevieve for a moment before she started the truck. She took in her light blue eyes and her Kewpie doll lips. She couldn't wait to get her home.

They pulled into Crockett's driveway and she was out of the truck and around to Genevieve's side before she had her door open. She opened Genevieve's door for her and helped her out of the truck. Crockett pulled her close against her when she was out of the truck.

Crockett walked Genevieve up the walkway that led to the front door. She opened the door and, once she'd closed it behind them, Genevieve moved into her arms. She ran her hands along Crockett's shoulders and linked her fingers behind her neck. Crockett wrapped her arms around Genevieve and pulled her close.

They kissed then, briefly and tenderly at first. But as the passion overwhelmed Crockett, she pressed Genevieve into her and ground against her. She needed her and wanted her. And she was about to have her. She ran her hands over Genevieve's full hips and around to cup her ass. Her head was about to explode from her desire. She broke the kiss and stood, breathless, in front of Genevieve.

While Crockett struggled to catch her breath, Genevieve began undressing.

"You don't have to do that here," Crockett said. "I do have a bedroom, you know."

"But I want you here and now."

What had happened to shy, innocent Genevieve? Crockett didn't care. She liked this wanton woman standing naked before her. She quickly removed her own clothes and pulled Genevieve to her again. The feel of her soft flesh against her own made her clit twitch. She walked Genevieve back to the couch and eased her down on it. She climbed on top of her and brought her knee up to press it into Genevieve's center. She was so warm and wet and ready for Crockett.

Genevieve rubbed against Crockett's knee, fueling the fire inside her. She wanted to take her completely, but didn't know if she'd be able to on the couch.

"You sure you wouldn't rather be in the bed?" Crockett asked, not sure she could wait that long.

"I don't want to wait another minute. Touch me, Crockett."

Crockett touched her then. She expertly stroked Genevieve's slick clit until she cried out as the first round of orgasms hit. But Crockett wasn't through. She slid her fingers inside her as deep as she could get. She plunged them in and out until Genevieve was breathing raggedly. Crockett stretched her thumb out and rubbed Genevieve's clit while she fucked her until Genevieve clamped down around her as her climax racked her body.

"Okay," Genevieve said when she'd caught her breath. "Now we can go to the bed."

Crockett climbed off her and helped her to her feet. She led her down the hall to her bedroom. She allowed Genevieve to climb into bed first and then joined her. She climbed between her legs and tasted the remnants of her orgasms. She ran her tongue over her and in her until Genevieve let out another moan letting Crockett know she'd been successful once again.

She climbed up next to Genevieve and moved to put her arms around her.

"Oh, no you don't," Genevieve said. "It's my turn. I get to play with your luscious body."

"I'm not going to argue with that."

Genevieve ran her hand down Crockett's body, stopping to tease her nipples. Crockett drew in a sharp intake of air. If Genevieve kept that up, Crockett would be a goner before the fun even started.

"You like that, huh?" Genevieve grinned.

"Oh, God, yes."

"Mm. Let's see what else you like."

She dragged her hand between Crockett's legs and lazily ran it over all she found. Crockett gritted her teeth to keep from telling her to hurry up. She had her so close and Crockett just wanted relief.

Genevieve finally dipped her fingers inside Crockett. She moved them in and out. Crockett arched off the bed to meet each thrust. Then Genevieve ran her hand over Crockett's clit and that's all it took. Crockett's world exploded into colors as she rode the wave of her orgasm.

They fell asleep finally, and when they woke the next morning, they did it all again. Crockett made Genevieve come over and over. She was so easy to please and so much fun to play with. And then Genevieve returned the favor. When they'd had enough, they showered together, where Crockett decided she hadn't really had enough. She washed Genevieve thoroughly, then ran her hands between her legs to coax another climax out of her.

The fun over, Crockett wasn't sure what to do.

"You want to go grab some breakfast or something?" she said.

"That would be great."

They went to the Italian Cottage and Crockett bought breakfast for both of them. After, Crockett followed Genevieve's directions and took her home.

"You're not going to ask for my phone number or anything, are you?" Genevieve sounded so hurt, but wouldn't it be worse to ask for it and never call?

"Look, Genevieve, last night was fun…"

"Yes, it was. But that's all it was. I get it."

"I'm sorry."

"No. I'm a big girl. I can handle one-night stands."

"Thanks."

"No problem. Thanks for breakfast," Genevieve said.

"You're welcome."

"See you around?"

"Definitely."

Crockett felt like a heel when she got home, but she didn't want to lead Genevieve on. And she was a nice, pretty, and smart woman. Someone more deserving would surely snatch her up.

CHAPTER FOUR

Gina was unpacking boxes the following Friday afternoon when she heard a knock on her door. Her first instinct was to ignore it, but whoever it was knocked again. Who could possibly be at her apartment at five o'clock on a Friday? She felt grimy and gross. She hadn't even taken a shower yet.

"Hold on!" she finally called. "I'm coming."

She opened the door to see Donna smiling at her with a six-pack of beer in one hand and a bottle of wine in the other.

"Housewarming gifts," she said.

"Donna..."

"Before you 'Donna' me, I come as a friend. I came to take you to dinner and dancing. I'm not here to seduce you."

Gina stared at her. She wasn't sure she was comfortable with Donna just showing up.

"I would have called, but you didn't give me your number," Donna continued.

Gina let out a sigh.

"Come in," she said and moved out of the way to allow Donna entrance.

"So, outside of me, how many visitors have you had here?"

"You're it."

"See? It's good to have a friend."

"But I don't want anything more than that."

"Neither do I. Would I mind hooking up with you again? Hell no, but do I want a relationship? Even bigger hell no."

Gina had to laugh. Donna was fun to be around. And the sex was good, but she didn't want a girlfriend. And she didn't want to lead Donna on. It didn't seem like she would be.

"Here," Gina said. "Let me put those beers in the fridge."

"Let me grab one first. And can I pour you a glass of wine?"

"I'll get it."

Gina took a wineglass out of the cupboard and poured herself some of the Malbec.

"I've never had this before."

"It's really good. I hope you like it."

"Please," Gina said. "Have a seat."

Donna sat on the couch and Gina sat in the loveseat across from her.

"So, you haven't answered me," Donna said. "Dinner and dancing tonight?"

"You promise you won't be led on?"

"I promise. We'll just have some fun. Sound good?"

"Okay. It'll be good to get out of this apartment, anyway."

"Good. How's the wine?"

"It's really good. Thanks for bringing it over."

"No problem. So I'm thinking Fifth Street Steak House for dinner. What do you think?"

"I have no idea. It sounds good, though."

"It is good. I mean, if you're a steak eater."

"I don't mind a good steak once in a while."

"Excellent. So we'll eat and then dance it off," Donna said.

"And then?" Gina was curious what, exactly, Donna had planned for later.

"Let the chips fall where they may."

"I see."

"Look, Gina. You seriously need to relax. What's wrong with having a friend with benefits?"

"Because that kind of relationship never works. One ends up falling for the other and someone gets hurt."

"Well," Donna said. "I'm not going to fall for you. Sorry, but I'm not the falling for type. And I promise to be just enough of a jerk that you won't fall for me, either."

Gina laughed.

"Okay," she said. "That sounds fair."

She finished her wine.

"Would you like another glass of wine?" Donna said.

"Actually, what I'd like is a shower."

"Would you like some company?"

"No, thank you. Not right now. Now, help yourself to another beer and I'll be out in a few."

Gina took a longer shower than she'd planned to. The hot water felt good on her muscles, which were sore from unpacking. She washed the sweat and grime off her and took her time drying off. When she was dry, she put on a light green cotton sundress that fell halfway down her calf. She was comfortable, yet looked nice. She slipped on some sandals and walked back out to find Donna sitting there drinking her beer. She stood when Gina walked in.

"Holy Jesus, you look amazing," Donna said.

"What? It's just a sundress."

"Yeah, but the color is amazing with your olive skin."

"Maybe it's just a shock because I looked so grimy when you first arrived."

"I don't know about that." Donna looked around. "So, it seems like there are less boxes here than the last time I was here."

"Yeah. I'm making progress. Slowly, but surely."

"You never told me, what brought you to Chico?"

"I'm a graduate student."

"Oh, that's right. You did tell me that. My bad. Good for you. I got my undergraduate, but never went any further."

"Really? You went to school so you could pour concrete?"

"Sure. I majored in construction management. I will be a fore-woman on a crew someday."

"Good for you."

"Yep. I can't wait. So, what's your degree in?"

"English."

"Wow. I barely speak it. I can't imagine majoring in it."

Gina laughed.

"It's not that hard. But I love the English language. And you're no slouch."

"Thank you."

They laughed together. Donna was so easy to be around. It felt good to have a friend. And the idea that she might get laid again certainly was appealing to Gina. She poured herself another glass of wine.

"Do you not have a television?" Donna asked as she looked around.

"No. I didn't bring one. I suppose I'll have to buy one. I don't watch a lot of TV. And I should be too busy with my studies to watch any. I prefer to read anyway. So, maybe I won't have to buy one after all."

"I have a spare. I'll bring it over to you. If you never watch it, no biggie, but this way at least you will have one."

"That's not necessary."

"I'm serious. It's sitting in my garage. Now, it's not all state-of-the-art or anything, but it's flat screen and has a good picture."

"Okay. If you insist."

"I do. Okay. That's settled."

"Yes," Gina said. "I suppose it is."

They finished their drinks.

"You ready for dinner?" Donna said.

Gina realized she hadn't eaten all day. No wonder the wine had given her a slight buzz.

"Yes," she said. "I'm famished. And a little buzzed. Do you mind driving?"

"Not at all." Donna smiled. "Come on."

They got into Donna's truck and drove to the restaurant. Gina had more wine before and during her meal. She was feeling no pain by the time they finished their meal and drove to the club.

"So, what are the rules here?" Donna said.

"What do you mean?"

"I mean, can we dance with other people tonight, or what?"

"I don't care if you do. But I figure you brought me, so I should dance with you only."

"I feel the same way. Okay. Glad that's settled. Now, let's go in."

Gina felt Donna's hand on the small of her back as they walked into the club. She thought that was fair. They were together that night. And Gina had decided to be okay with that. They found a table and Donna went to the bar to get them drinks. Gina surveyed the room and almost immediately, she saw the blonde. She was facing away from Gina, but she would recognize that ass, the toned arms, and the short, croppy hair anywhere. The woman turned around and looked Gina's way but, once again, seemed to look right past her. What was it with her anyway, Gina wondered.

Donna was back with their drinks. The music was blaring and the beat coursed through Gina's body.

"Let's dance," she said.

She led Donna to the floor. She cut right past the blonde, who still seemed not to notice her. Oh well, this night was about Donna. Another time, Gina would ask the blonde to dance and see where that would take them.

Donna and Gina danced for several hours, through fast songs and slow songs. Finally, Donna pleaded exhaustion.

"Can we get out of here?" she said.

"Sure," Gina said. Her blood was pumping after all that dancing and she was ready to dance horizontally with Donna.

Donna drove them back to Gina's apartment, and when Gina had let them inside, Donna took Gina in her arms.

"Didn't you want another beer or anything?" Gina asked.

"No," Donna said. "All I want is you."

She kissed Gina, hard, and Gina's toes curled. She enjoyed the way Donna kissed, soft, yet passionately. Hard, but gentle. She couldn't really describe it, but she liked it.

They stumbled down the hallway, undressing each other as they went. By the time they fell into bed, they were both naked. Donna wasted no time kissing down Gina's body. She placed Gina's knees over her own shoulders and buried her face between Gina's legs. She devoured everything she found there and took little time before bringing to Gina to an exquisite orgasm.

After, Donna held Gina as they slept.

❖

Crockett danced with several women that night. She was restless and none of them really seemed to call to her to take them home. Finally, she found a cherubic brunette who made her crotch clench. She was beautiful and Crockett quickly crossed the club to talk to her.

"Hi," she said.

"Hi." The woman smiled at her.

"Would you like to dance?"

"Sure."

They danced several songs until they both needed something to drink.

"What are you drinking?" Crockett asked.

"Whiskey Sour."

"Okay. I'll go get you one."

"Thank you."

Crockett came back with their drinks. She extended her hand to the woman.

"I'm Crockett," she said.

"I'm Toni."

"Nice to meet you, Toni."

"Nice to meet you, too."

"Do you want to dance some more?"

"Okay."

They went back to the floor and danced together for several more songs. Crockett was enjoying watching Toni's body move to the music, but she wanted more. She took her hand and led her back to the table.

"You want another drink?" Crockett said.

"No, thanks, I'm fine."

"Okay. Well, I guess I'll say good night then."

"Why? The night is young," Toni said.

"But if you don't want another drink…"

"Not here. I'm sure you have something to drink at your place, though, right?"

Crockett smiled. She liked Toni's directness.

"Sure I do." She offered her elbow. "Let's go."

Toni slid her hand through Crockett's elbow and they left the club together.

"Do you want to follow me home?" Crockett said.

"I don't have a car. Can't I get a ride with you?"

Crockett didn't like that. That meant no early morning departure. Oh, well. She could give Toni a ride home. If that was the price she had to pay for a roll in the hay with her, it would be worth it.

"Sure," Crockett said. "You can get a ride with me. Come on."

They got back to Crockett's house and Crockett offered Toni a drink.

"Sure. What do you have?"

"I have pretty much anything you want. You want a whiskey sour?"

"Please."

Crockett put her bartending skills to good use and whipped up a drink for Toni. She grabbed a beer for herself. They sat together on her couch. She slipped her arm around Toni.

"I like your house," Toni said.

"Thanks. It's home."

Toni moved closer to Crockett. Crockett liked the feel of Toni against her. She sipped her beer while silently cursing the delay that was keeping them apart. She was ready for Toni. She could tell Toni was going to be a lot of fun in bed. She just sensed it. But Toni didn't seem to be in any hurry as she sipped the drink Crockett had made for her.

Crockett moved in to kiss Toni and Toni let her. The kiss was tentative, obviously a first kiss, but it sent shocks through Crockett's body. She pulled away and Toni sat staring at Crockett's lips for a few moments before she took another sip of her drink.

"That was nice," she said.

"Yeah, it was. Are you almost through with that drink?" Crockett was losing her patience.

"Almost." Toni smiled.

"Okay." Crockett set her empty beer bottle on the coffee table and leaned back with her arm around Toni again. Finally, Toni set her empty glass next to Crockett's bottle.

"Would you like a refill?" Crockett asked, every bone in her body hoping Toni would say no.

"No, thank you."

"Good." Crockett leaned into Toni and kissed her again. She eased her back on the couch and climbed on top of her as they continued to kiss. Suddenly aware of where she was, Crockett sat up. "I'm sorry. I was about to have you right here on the couch."

"I wouldn't mind." Toni pulled Crockett back down.

They continued to kiss until Crockett was light-headed with need.

"Come on." She got off Toni. "Let's go to my room."

They quickly undressed and climbed into bed. Crockett reached her hand between Toni's legs and found her wet and ready. She plunged her fingers deep inside her and twisted them back and forth while she moved them in and out.

Toni arched to meet her thrusts and made little mewling sounds which let Crockett know she was close. Crockett kissed down Toni's body, stopping to suck on each hard nipple for a few minutes. Toni was moaning by that point, her need for release apparent. Crockett ended up between Toni's legs. She took her swollen clit in her mouth and sucked on it while she played over it with her tongue. Toni pressed Crockett's face against her. Crockett could barely breathe, but she kept at it until Toni screamed and Crockett felt her insides clenching around her fingers.

Crockett kept at it and Toni came several more times.

"Okay," Toni finally said. "No more. Come here. It's your turn."

Crockett wasn't about to argue that, as she was wet and swollen and ready to climax herself.

Toni reached between Crockett's legs and stroked her clit. There was no warm-up, no nothing. She just went for it. But that was okay by Crockett, who cried out as her orgasm rocked her.

She held Toni as they slept, and Crockett awoke the next morning to Toni's fingers inside her, exploring.

"Well, good morning to me," she said.

"I wanted to play with you more today. Last night, I just wanted to get you off."

"Fair enough. Play away."

Toni did just that. She moved her fingers in and out of Crockett before she moved them to her clit, which by then was rock hard. She sucked on Crockett's nipples as she rubbed her clit.

Crockett felt the ball of energy coalesce in her center. She closed her eyes and focused only on what Toni was doing to her. Soon, the ball of energy burst open, shooting hot currents throughout her body as the orgasm cascaded over her.

When she'd floated back to earth, Crockett took her time with Toni, bringing her over the edge several more times.

"You sure know what you're doing in bed," Toni said.

"Thanks. So do you."

Toni blushed.

"I do okay. But you? Damn."

Crockett just laughed.

"So, how about a shower?" Crockett said.

"No. I think I'd better just get dressed so you can take me home."

Crockett didn't act disappointed. She was fine if Toni wanted to go home. It made life easier for her.

"Sure. We can do that," she said.

They dressed in silence and then Crockett drove Toni home. The ride was uncomfortable to Crockett, but she didn't know what to say, so she didn't say anything. The only conversation was when Toni would give directions.

Once Toni was dropped off, Crockett drove home, showered, and called Melinda. There was no answer. No biggie, thought Crockett. She had homework to grade and finals to prepare for. There were only a couple of weeks left in summer session. The fall semester would be starting soon and she wanted to be ready.

Chapter Five

G ina enjoyed her morning by the pool, but by one she was restless. She still had boxes to unpack, but she was anxious to get school started. She had received her schedule the day before. She decided it was time to head over to the university.

She took a shower and dressed in shorts and a green spaghetti strapped shirt and walked the six blocks to campus. It was hot, unbelievably hot, but at least there was no humidity like the Midwest.

Gina found Siskiyou Hall easily once she was on campus. It was close to the center of town, on the edge of the campus. She walked through the hall and found her classrooms. She noted that she was a teaching assistant for a Melinda O'Neill. She wondered if she would be around. She wanted to introduce herself and maybe get a syllabus for the coming semester, so she'd be able to prepare for it.

She found her office and noted her office hours weren't for another hour. Gina decided to wander around campus until then. She found a little eatery and ordered a sandwich and iced coffee and took it to a picnic table down by the creek to enjoy. The area was shaded and somewhat cooler than the rest of the campus. She thought about going to the bookstore and buying her books for her classes, but really wanted to meet her professor first. She didn't want to lug around a bunch of books. She'd drive over and buy them later.

Gina checked her watch. Almost time to meet Professor O'Neill. She threw her garbage away and straightened her clothes. She ran her hand over her hair. She wanted to make a good impression.

She walked back across campus to Siskiyou Hall. She found Professor O'Neill's door opened. There were butterflies in her stomach. She'd never TA'd before, but was looking forward to the opportunity. She knocked on the open door and poked her head in. The woman with the shoulder-length red hair sitting behind the desk in the cramped quarters looked vaguely familiar. She couldn't place her, though.

"Hello?" Melinda looked up.

"Hi, Professor O'Neill. I'm Gina Moreno. I'll be a TA in Creative Writing this semester. I just wanted to meet you before school started."

"Well, hello, Gina." Melinda stood and offered her hand. "And please call me Melinda."

"Thanks, Melinda."

"How is it I have a TA that's never been in one of my classes before?"

"I'm a transfer student. I'm here in the graduate program."

"Oh, well, welcome to Chico State."

"Thank you. I can't wait to start classes."

"Good. You still have a few weeks, though."

"Yes," Gina said. "I know."

"Well, great. I'm so glad you stopped by so we could meet."

"I was wondering," Gina said. "Do you have a book list of anything you'll be assigning to the class that I may be able to buy early so I can get a head start?"

"Sure. I have one here somewhere. Let me think."

While Melinda was looking, a voice from the doorway called out.

"Professor O'Neill?"

Gina turned as Melinda looked up and saw the hot blonde she'd been lusting after standing in the doorway. Right there in front of her. Close enough to touch. Up close she could see the deep blue of her eyes.

The offices were barely large enough for the desk and the professor. Add another person and they were cramped. And now that the blonde was there, the air seemed to go out of the room. She wanted to escape, but there was nowhere to go. Why was she reacting this way? She was a grown woman.

"Professor Crockett Devine," Melinda said. "This is my TA for Creative Writing this semester, Gina Moreno."

"Nice to meet you." Crockett held out her hand.

"Nice to meet you too, Professor."

They held hands a little too long. Gina could feel heat rising in her cheeks.

"Please call me Crockett. You look vaguely familiar. Have you been in one of my classes?" Crockett said.

"No," Melinda said. "She's a transfer student. But I agree. She does look familiar."

"Sorry," Gina said. "I'm new to town."

"Well, welcome," Crockett said. "I'll come back later."

"Oh, no," Gina said, taking a sheet Melinda had handed to her. "I was just on my way out. Thanks again, Melinda. I'll see you soon."

She walked out of the office, brushing into Crockett on her way out. Her whole body felt alive with electrical current as she walked down the hall and out into the fresh air.

Crockett watched Gina hurry down the hallway.

"She seemed like she couldn't wait to get out of here," Crockett said.

"She probably didn't want to interrupt us."

"Maybe…"

"What?" Melinda said.

"What, what?"

"You're in a daze over her? She's not really your type."

"I swear I've seen her before."

"I don't know what to tell you. Now, to what do I owe this pleasure?"

"Hm?"

"Your visit to my office," Melinda said. "Jesus, woman, what's with you?"

"I don't know. That woman…"

"Gina."

"Yeah, Gina. Something about her really caught my attention."

"Okay, but that's not why you came to my office originally, was it? To meet her?"

"No. I came to see if you and Terry want to go to the club Friday night."

"Sure. That would be fun."

"Great, and I'll buy dinner beforehand."

"Sounds good," Melinda said.

"Cool. I'll see you then, if not before."

She left Melinda's office and went to her own. There was plenty for her to do there, but she couldn't get her mind off Gina. She had beautiful olive skin and almond shaped dark brown eyes. Her smile seemed nervous, like she was afraid of something, but nothing Crockett could know of, obviously. Her body was lean and tight and her breasts a beautiful size, a bit large for the rest of her body. No, she wasn't Crockett's type, so why couldn't Crockett get her out of her mind?

Friday night rolled around and Crockett met Melinda and Terry at the restaurant.

"You two ready for some fun tonight?" Crockett said.

"Of course," Melinda said. "Are you?"

"You know it. I can't wait to get my groove on. I'm so glad you two like to dance. It gets old going there by myself."

"You can always invite us," Terry said. "We don't normally go out on weekends, so we're usually available."

"Excellent. I just keep trying to make a good impression on you, Terry, and chasing skirts at a club probably isn't the best way to do that."

Terry laughed.

"Nonsense. There's much more to you than simply chasing skirts. Although I do find it amusing to watch you in action. Even though Melinda had warned me, you're very skilled at what you do."

"Thank you?"

"You may take it as a compliment. Some day you'll be ready to settle down. But until then, live it up, I say."

"Good. I'm glad I don't disgust you."

"Not at all."

They ate their meal and kept the conversation light and fun. By the time they were ready to go to the club, Crockett was more than ready to find a woman to bed for the evening. Her hormones had been on alert ever since meeting that Gina woman, and she wanted to find someone to make her forget about her. She was her best friend's TA, after all.

They met in the parking lot and walked in together. Crockett surveyed the place. Lots of women. Good. That meant lots of chances. She had Terry and Melinda choose a table while she went to get the drinks from the bar. When she got back, she sat with them and sipped her beer. The music was playing and her foot was tapping. She started bobbing her head. It was time to dance.

She looked around and saw one woman who looked good to her. She made her way over and asked her to dance. The woman agreed, but when Crockett reached for her hand, she pulled it away. Whatever, Crockett thought.

They got on the dance floor and the woman could really dance. They danced one song, but before Crockett could ask for another, the woman had left the floor and was walking back toward her friends. Crockett walked back to her table.

"Well, that didn't go too well, did it?" Melinda said.

"That's okay. There are plenty more women here."

And it was true. In the short time Crockett had been dancing, the place had really filled up. There were wall-to-wall women. Just how she liked it.

She scanned the room again, focusing on the tables in the elevated area. Suddenly, her gaze stopped. She slapped Melinda on the arm.

"Ouch," Melinda said. "What was that for?"

"She's here."

"Who's here?"

"Look."

Melinda turned and followed Crockett's gaze. There sat Gina with a middle-aged woman with a long, dark braid hanging down her back.

"No wonder she looked familiar," Melinda said.

"Do you think they're together?" Crockett said.

"There's only one way to find out."

"It looks like she's drinking a chocolate martini. I'm going to take her one."

"What about her friend?"

"Oh, yeah. Okay. I'll just go up there like an idiot and ask if they're together."

"You can't do that either." Melinda laughed.

"Shit."

"What is with you? Like I said, she's not even your type."

"I know. I don't know, but I've got to take a chance with her."

Crockett finished her beer and made her way up to Gina's table. Gina and her friend were facing the other way, watching the dancers.

"No wonder you look familiar," Crockett said to announce herself.

Gina and her friend both turned. Crockett thought she saw pink on Gina's cheeks.

"Hi, Crockett. Fancy meeting you here."

"Hi, Gina. And hi, Brenda. I didn't recognize you from across the bar."

"Hi, Crockett," Brenda said. "Would you care to join us?"

"If you don't mind. But how about I go get us some drinks first?"

"Sure. I'll take another beer," Brenda said.

"And I'll have a chocolate martini."

"Coming right up."

As she walked off, Crockett could swear she felt Gina's gaze burning into her. She walked by Terry and Melinda.

"I'll be sitting up there for a while," she said and winked.

"Enjoy," they said together.

Crockett got the drinks and made her way back to their table. It was crowded in that section and when she sat, her leg was pressed into Gina's. She felt sparks flying and wondered if Gina felt them, too. If she did, she didn't let on.

"So, how do you two know each other?" Brenda said.

"I'm a TA for Melinda O'Neill next semester, and I met Crockett while I was in her office for a quick meet and greet."

"Ah, yes," Brenda said. "Melinda and Crockett are thick as thieves."

"Is that right?" Gina arched an eyebrow at Crockett.

"Pretty much. So, plan on seeing a lot of me."

"Sounds like a plan," Gina said.

What did that mean? Crockett searched for something intelligent to say.

"So, what brings you two out on a Friday night?" Crockett winced internally. Real original.

"Since Gina here is new and I'm newly single, we occasionally accompany each other to the club. Just so we don't have to go alone."

"Very cool. That works."

They sat there for a few moments in silence and sipped their drinks.

"Would you like to dance, Gina?" Crockett finally worked up the nerve to ask.

"Sure."

Crockett stood and let Gina lead the way to the floor. They ended up dancing right next to Melinda and Terry.

"Hi, Gina," Melinda called above the music.

"Hi, Melinda. It's good to see you again."

"You, too. This is my girlfriend, Terry."

"Nice to meet you."

Crockett watched the exchange unhappily. Sure, it was great that they were all friendly and enjoying themselves, but she wanted to watch Gina get into the music, not talk. The song ended.

"Another one?" Crockett asked.

"Why not?"

This time Gina lost herself in the music, and Crockett moved with her, loving watching her body moving so fluidly. She was a natural and Crockett thought she was probably a natural in bed, too. But even as desperately as she wanted to take her home, she knew she'd better tread gently with this one. She didn't know why. Something just told her.

They walked back to the table when the song ended. They finished their drinks.

"Can I buy another round?" Crockett said.

"Not for me," Gina said. "I should get going."

Crockett didn't try to hide her disappointment.

"Really?"

"Yeah."

"Well, can I take you out tomorrow night? Dinner and more dancing?"

"Sure. And I promise to get lots of rest so I'll be able to stay out later."

"That would be great."

Crockett handed Gina her phone.

"Go ahead and enter your number."

Gina did and handed the phone back to Crockett.

"I sleep late, though, so please don't call before noon."

"I wouldn't dream of it," Crockett said.

She stood and watched Brenda and Gina leave the club. She took her beer and went back to her original table. Terry and Melinda were on the floor again. She was jealous. She was about to get another beer and lick her wounds when she heard a familiar voice in her ear.

"You want to dance?"

She turned to see Gabby standing there. Her mood lightened.

"Sure," she said.

They went out on the floor and moved and grooved through several songs. When a slow song came on, Gabby moved into Crockett's arms. Crockett held her as they danced. When the dance ended, Gabby suggested they get out of here.

"You know," Crockett said. "I'm not looking for a relationship."

"Just because people sleep together a couple of times, it doesn't mean they're in a relationship," Gabby said.

"Excellent answer."

Gabby followed Crockett back to her house and they picked up where they'd left off the time before. Clothes were shed, nipples were sucked and pinched and twisted. Flesh was pressed against flesh. Tongues were entwined. And through it all, Crockett fought to keep her mind focused on Gabby and off Gina.

Finally, when she was between Gabby's legs, she was successful at devoting her full attention to Gabby as she brought her to her climax. Her tongue and fingers were cramping when she finally took Gabby over the edge another time.

But when it was Gabby's turn to have her, she fantasized that it was Gina who had her hands on her, Gina who was deep inside her. She thought of Gina's long, slender fingers rubbing her swollen clit until she came.

They awoke the next morning and Crockett felt slightly guilty. She felt like she'd cheated on Gina. She didn't know why. She hadn't even dated her, much less slept with her. She'd left the club early. Crockett had no ties on her.

To prove it to herself, she took Gabby again and again that morning, until Gabby complained she'd never be able to walk again if Crockett didn't stop. So, Crockett stopped and let Gabby have a turn at her. She made Crockett come powerfully and completely.

After they were through, Gabby reached for her clothes.

"That was fun. Thanks."

"Thank you. It was just what I needed."

Crockett said good-bye to Gabby then jumped in the shower. She put on some old shorts and a torn T-shirt and made breakfast and fed Archie. Then she settled in front of the television, just waiting for noon to arrive. She figured she'd wait until one so she didn't look too anxious. But that last hour was a killer. Finally, she picked up the phone and dialed.

CHAPTER SIX

Gina woke up around ten on Saturday. She stretched and moaned and wondered what she'd do that day. Then she remembered. She had a date with Crockett. She climbed out of bed and smiled. Crockett. The blond woman she'd lusted after for so long. She had a date with her. Wow. She could hardly believe her luck. She'd felt bad for leaving the night before, but she'd promised Brenda it would be an early night. And she'd driven, so she really didn't have a choice. But that night? That night, the sky was the limit. And she hoped to reach that limit many times over.

She unpacked some more boxes, keeping her eye on the clock the whole time. Why had she told Crockett not to call before noon? She wanted to talk to her then. She didn't want to wait. And then noon came and went. Had Crockett changed her mind? Oh, she hoped not. She hoped with every ounce of her being Crockett still wanted to go out with her.

The phone rang and she nearly jumped out of her skin. She told herself to be cool.

"Hello?" she said.

"Hi. Gina?"

Gina immediately recognized the voice on the other end. Deep and velvety and sexy as hell.

"Hi, Crockett," she said.

"Hey. How are you this afternoon?"

"I'm great, and you?"

"Not bad."

"Good," Gina said.

"So, I was calling about tonight."

"Okay."

"I thought I'd pick you up at seven and we can go get dinner. Then go dancing afterward. How does that sound?"

"That sounds wonderful. I'll be ready at seven."

"And where do you live?"

Gina gave her the address of her apartment.

"So, I'll see you tonight, then?" Gina said.

"You'd better believe it."

Gina smiled.

"Okay. Good-bye, Crockett."

"Good-bye, Gina."

Gina set her phone on the table and collapsed on to the couch. She smiled widely. She was going out with Crockett Devine, quite possibly the hottest woman she'd ever seen. She was beside herself with excitement. And she still had almost six hours to wait until Crockett arrived.

She set to work unpacking boxes in her living room, so it would be less embarrassing when Crockett showed up. She was getting there, slowly, but surely. But she didn't want to overdo it that day. She didn't want to be tired that night. Oh, no, she had big plans for the upcoming evening and she wanted to be wide awake for it.

Gina was sitting on the couch drinking a diet soda when there was a knock on the door. She glanced at the clock. It was only five. Surely Crockett wouldn't come by two hours early. Not without calling. She stood and smoothed her dirty clothes and tried to smooth her sweaty hair. She opened the door.

There stood Donna carrying a six-pack of beer and a bottle of wine.

"Hello there," she said. "Who wants to go out tonight?"

Gina stood there, dumbfounded. Maybe it was time to give Donna her phone number to avoid this from happening.

"Hey, Donna. It's good to see you. But I can't go out with you tonight. I already have a date."

"You do, huh? That's great. So you're getting out there and meeting people. That's fantastic."

Gina watched Donna's face for signs of disappointment, but she seemed fine with Gina having a date.

"You want to come in and have a beer?" Gina offered. "I have a few minutes before I have to get ready."

"No. That's okay. I'll take off. But can I get your number, so I can call you instead of just rudely showing up at your doorstep?"

"You're never rude, Donna."

They exchanged phones and entered their number into the other's phone. When that was done, Donna handed Gina the beer and wine.

"Here," she said. "In case you end up back here tonight. You'll have something to offer her to drink."

"Thanks, Donna. That's sweet of you."

"My pleasure. Look, you have fun tonight, okay?"

"I will. Maybe I'll see you out and about."

"I'm goin' to the club, so if you're headed that way, I'm sure we'll see each other."

"Great. Well, have fun," Gina said.

"Thanks. You, too."

Gina watched Donna get into her truck and drive off. Well, she thought, if there was any doubt in Donna's mind about them seeing each other exclusively, that was taken care of now.

Gina went inside and poured herself a glass of wine and settled into the large bath in the master bathroom. She'd filled the bath with lavender and vanilla scented oils. She relaxed into the scents and sipped her wine. She was so relaxed she almost fell asleep. She realized it was six fifteen and she needed to get a move on if Crockett was going to be there in forty-five minutes.

She got out of the tub and showered off. She felt nice and clean. She stepped into a tan cotton sundress and slipped on some sandals. She hadn't noticed how tall Crockett was, so she chose flats to hopefully make her shorter than Crockett. She brushed her hair until it shone and poured another glass of wine. She sat on her couch and watched the clock slowly tick off minutes.

At precisely seven o'clock, there was a knock on her door. She told the butterflies in her stomach to calm down as she set down her wine, smoothed her dress, and made her way to the door. She opened the door to see Crockett standing there with flowers in her hand.

"Here," Crockett said. "These are for you."

Gina took them and smelled them.

"They're beautiful. Please, won't you come in?"

She stepped aside and let Crockett enter. She checked out her firm ass under her cargo shorts and felt her clit twitch.

"I'll just put these in some water," she said. "Would you like a beer?"

"Sure. That would be great."

Gina was very aware of Crockett's gaze on her as she found the vase and put the flowers in it. Then she got a beer for Crockett out of the fridge and handed it to her.

"I was just having a glass of wine in here."

She led Crockett to the living room.

"These are nice apartments," Crockett said. "Are they new? I don't remember seeing them here before."

"I honestly don't know. They seem fairly new though."

Crockett nodded.

"You like living here?"

"I've only been here a month or so. But yeah, so far it's nice. I like that it's only a few blocks from school so I can walk if I want."

"Chico's a great town for walking."

"It just seems like a great town overall. I think I've made the right decision."

"Good. I'm glad to hear that."

They finished their drinks. Crockett stood.

"So, I'm thinking Thai food. Does that work for you?"

"Sure. That will be great."

"Excellent."

Crockett held the door open and Gina walked past her, careful to bump against her as she did. She felt the shocks coursing through her body again. Her response to Crockett was so intense, so visceral. She wondered how the night would end.

Crockett led the way to her truck and helped Gina in. The feel of Crockett's hand on her made her weak in the knees, and she was happy she could hold herself together to gracefully get in and sit down.

The restaurant was downtown, not far from the university. They ordered and then chatted.

"So, why Chico State?" Crockett asked.

"Everything about it spoke to me. It has an excellent English department. It's in a small town and I've always loved the idea of Northern California."

"All those things are true. Well, I for one, am glad you chose it."

She raised her glass in a toast.

"Me, too." Gina raised her glass as well.

They kept up a pleasant conversation through dinner, and finally, it was time to go dancing. Gina had enjoyed dancing with Crockett the night before, and tonight, with no time restraints? Who knew how things might play out?

The club was full by the time they got there.

"Wow," Gina said. "This is quite a crowd."

"Yeah, well, it is Saturday night, after all."

"Yes, it is."

"Let's go look for a table," Crockett said.

They found the last available one in the elevated area. Crockett pulled her chair out for Gina to sit.

"You stay here. I'll go get us drinks. A chocolate martini?"

"Please." Gina smiled. She was happy Crockett had remembered what she drank.

Gina surveyed the crowd while she was waiting for Crockett to get back. She was starting to recognize some of the same faces she'd seen before. Not all of them. There were too many for that, but a few started to look familiar.

"I thought you had a date," Donna said as she sat in Crockett's chair.

"I do. She's getting our drinks."

"Oh, okay. I won't stay long. You look amazing tonight."

"Thank you. You're not so bad yourself."

Donna wore carpenter jeans with a blue button-up oxford shirt.

"Thanks."

Just then, Crockett walked up with their drinks. Donna stood.

"Crockett," she said.

"Good to see you, Donna. I see you've met Gina?"

"Yeah. I know Gina."

"You're welcome to join us if you want," Crockett said.

"No, thanks. I'm flying solo tonight. But I might be back to visit later."

"Sounds good."

Gina watched Donna move through the crowd. She really hoped Donna didn't have feelings for her. She would have just hurt her if she did. No, she told herself. They'd discussed it. They'd slept together a few times. That was all. Now, all her attention was going to be on Crockett.

She took a sip of her martini.

"They make the best chocolate martinis here," she said.

"Good," Crockett replied, "I can't imagine drinking anything that froufy."

Gina laughed. She couldn't imagine it either. Crockett laughed with her. It was a wonderful sound that made her panties wet. It was low and light and suited her perfectly.

"You want to dance?" Crockett said into her ear.

Gina's nipples tightened at the feel of Crockett's breath on her. Her nearness made her tremble.

"Sure," she managed.

They were pressed together as they fought through the crowd on their way to the floor. Gina could barely breathe. She felt Crockett's slight breasts against her back, and the feeling was almost too much for her.

They found a spot on the floor and danced one song after another. Crockett was an excellent dancer, which Gina had kind of assumed. She wouldn't be at a dance club as often as she was if she couldn't dance. At least somewhat. But she could really move. And watching her move only fanned the flame already burning in Gina's center.

After several dances, they made their way back to their table and Crockett went to get them more drinks. Gina was hot, both from the dancing and from the company. She watched the women dance while she waited for Crockett to return. There were a lot of attractive women there, but none were as outright smokin' as Crockett. Gina considered herself a lucky woman that Crockett had asked her out. She was sure any femme in the club would give their right arm for a date with Crockett.

"You enjoying watching the dancers?" Crockett was back with their drinks.

Gina jumped a little. She'd been so lost in her thoughts, Crockett had startled her.

"Yes," Gina said. "I love the variety of women who come here."

"Yeah. It's a good melting pot."

"It really is."

They sipped their drinks in silence while each bobbed their heads to the music.

"Did you want to dance again?" Crockett said.

"I'd love to."

Crockett took her hand. Crockett's hand was strong and sure. Gina wanted her to hold her hand forever. They got to the center of the floor and Gina let the music take over her body. She loved moving to it, lost in it, only vaguely aware of Crockett.

Then the music slowed and Crockett opened her arms. Gina stepped into them and felt like she was finally home. When Crockett closed her arms around her, she felt at once aroused and at peace. It was the strangest sensation. One she didn't want to end. They moved as one, pressed together, and nothing else in the world mattered. Gina rested her head on Crockett's shoulder and Crockett's hands rested on the small of her back. Gina fought to maintain her balance as the sensations washed over her.

When the song ended, Gina was breathless.

"Did you want to sit the next song out?" Crockett asked.

"I want to get out of here."

"Are you sure?"

"I'm positive."

Crockett was bummed. She'd been having fun, but if Gina was ready to go home, then she'd take her. But before she said good night, she'd be sure to ask her out again. She'd had an awesome time that night. And she definitely planned to see Gina again.

They drove back to Gina's apartment. Crockett braced herself for good night.

"Did you want to come in for a nightcap?" Gina said.

"I'd love that." Crockett's heart leaped. She'd just assumed her date was over. Now she wondered how it might end for real. She could only hope.

They got out of the truck and Crockett reached for Gina's hand. She allowed her to take it. This was a good sign. When they got inside, Gina closed the door and turned to face Crockett. What was Crockett seeing in her eyes? Desire? Fatigue? She thought it was desire. She hoped it was. Crockett wanted her in the worst way. But she could wait. She didn't know what it was about Gina, but something about her was different. Just Gina's presence spoke to a part of Crockett in a way no woman had before.

"So, beer?" Gina said.

Was it Crockett's imagination or did Gina's voice shake a little? Was she scared?

"I'd love a beer."

"Go ahead and have a seat on the couch. I'll be right there."

Crockett sat down. She turned this way and that, trying to decide how to sit. Finally, she sat facing where Gina would sit and ran her arm along the back of the couch. Gina came in and handed Crockett a beer. She sat on the couch and snuggled next to Crockett. Crockett was happy. It felt good to have Gina so close.

"So, did you have a good time tonight?" Crockett asked.

"Do you really need to ask?"

Crockett laughed.

"You seemed to have fun. I'm just checking."

"I had a wonderful time."

Gina placed her hand on Crockett's leg. Crockett felt it burn from the heat between them. She wondered if Gina had any idea the effect she had on her. She wanted to shift just slightly so her hand would be under the leg of her shorts. But she didn't. That would be too crude. She tried to keep her hormones in check, but it wasn't easy. She was getting dizzy sitting as close as she was to Gina.

"So, I was wondering," Gina said.

"Yes?" Crockett focused hard on Gina's words. She was so aroused by her closeness, she was starting to float.

"Would you like to spend the night?"

Was she serious? Crockett felt her clit swell. She hadn't even kissed her yet and she was being asked to stay the night. She stared into Gina's eyes.

"Would you like me to?" she asked when she finally found her voice.

"Very much."

"Then that settles it. I'll stay the night."

Crockett took Gina's wine and set it on the coffee table. She set her beer next to it. She took Gina's hands in hers. She looked deep into her eyes. They were beautiful, soft pools of dark brown.

And in them she saw a hunger. A hunger Crockett swore to herself to appease.

She leaned in to Gina, closing the distance between them a millimeter at a time. She wanted to draw this out. It would be their first kiss and she wanted it to be right. She finally barely brushed Gina's lips with hers. Electricity coursed through her veins. And that was just from a light kiss.

Gina snaked her arms around Crockett and pulled her close. She kissed Crockett and ran her tongue along Crockett's lips. Crockett opened her mouth and welcomed Gina in. They kissed slowly, deliberately. Crockett was fighting a losing battle at keeping her head. She was so filled with desire, she had to have Gina. But again, she wanted everything to be right. For some reason, she didn't want a wham-bam-thank-you-ma'am night. She wanted a beginning of something.

CHAPTER SEVEN

Crockett kissed Gina for a long time, teasing herself as well as Gina. She was making them wait. Making sure they were both ready. She knew she was, but was Gina?

"Let's go to bed," Gina whispered.

"Are you ready?"

"Beyond."

Crockett stood and offered her hand to Gina, who slid her soft hand into it. Her skin was silky smooth, and Crockett couldn't wait to feel the rest of her. Something weird was going on inside Crockett. She couldn't put her finger on it, but she knew this night would be special. She was determined to make it so. For both of them.

Gina led them to her bedroom and Crockett stood, staring at the king-size bed in the center of the room. Sure, there were other things in the room. And maybe she should have looked at them and commented on them, but her focus was on the bed and all the promises it held.

Crockett pulled Gina to her and kissed her hard on her mouth. She ran her hands over her back and down to cup her shapely ass. She pressed her into herself, making her hormones rage. She finally broke the kiss and lifted Gina's dress over her head.

Gina stood there in matching black lace panties and bra. She took Crockett's breath away.

"You're beautiful," Crockett said.

"Thank you."

There was nothing shy or demure about the way she said it. She knew she was attractive in a way that only made her more so. Crockett reached around and unhooked Gina's bra. Her full breasts sprung free.

"Gorgeous," Crockett breathed. "Just gorgeous."

She held Gina's breasts in her hands and ran her thumbs over her nipples, feeling them harden at her touch. She bent and took a nipple in her mouth. She sucked hard on it and ran her tongue over its tip. The feeling was making her crazy and seemed to be driving Gina wild. Gina had her hands laced through Crockett's hair and was holding her in place.

Crockett moved to the other nipple and sucked it just as determinedly. She was lost in the sensation of sucking on Gina. Gina finally pulled her up to kiss her. Crockett kissed back with a fervor. She was losing control. Her need for Gina was overwhelming her.

She slid her hand down Gina's belly and ran her fingertips under the waistband of her panties. She felt Gina's skin ripple at her touch. She had gooseflesh on her own skin from her excitement. She slowly peeled Gina's panties off until Gina stood naked before her. She was a work of art.

"I don't know if I've ever seen anything as beautiful as you," Crockett said.

"You sure are a smooth talker."

"No, Gina. I mean it. You're beautiful. Indescribably so."

"Well, thank you. Now, let's get you out of your clothes."

Crockett moved to take her shirt off, but Gina stopped her.

"Oh, no," she said. "I get to undress you."

She stepped closer to Crockett and took Crockett's shirt off over her head. She pulled her undershirt off next so Crockett stood bare from the waist up. Gina stepped closer and pressed her breasts into Crockett while she fumbled with the button on her shorts.

Crockett fought to remain standing. The feel of Gina's breasts pressed into her was almost too much to bear. Gina got Crockett's shorts unbuttoned and unzipped and slipped them off her. Crockett stood in her boxers, wanting to take them off, but not knowing if that was something Gina planned on doing.

Gina slid her fingers inside the legs of Crockett's boxers. Crockett stepped back.

"Oh no you don't," she said. "Ladies first in my book."

Crockett stepped back and out of her boxers. She pulled Gina against her again, reveling in flesh against flesh. But this time, it was different. There was the white-hot electricity coursing through her as usual, but there was more. There was a deep ache, a deep connection that she couldn't explain, but didn't want to end.

She kissed Gina again and eased her back onto the bed. She climbed on top of her and ground her pelvis into Gina's. Gina wrapped her legs around Crockett. Crockett could feel the moist heat from her center radiating toward her. Crockett rolled off Gina and skimmed her hand up and down her body. She was indeed as silky and soft as her hands. Crockett couldn't wait to devour every inch of her.

Crockett sucked on Gina's nipples again. She took her time sucking them, pressing them into the roof of her mouth. When Gina was moaning, Crockett released her grip on her breasts and kissed lower down her body.

She nibbled on her soft skin and licked at her cute little belly button. She moved lower yet and finally ended up between Gina's legs. She took a moment to simply gaze at the feast before her.

"Oh, my God," she said. "You're beautiful everywhere."

"I'm glad you think so."

"Oh, I do."

Crockett inhaled deeply. The scent of Gina was intoxicating. She finally lowered her mouth and ran her tongue over every inch of her. She tasted like heaven—sweet and salty and musky and delicious. She dipped her tongue as far in Gina as she could and lapped at the juices flowing there. She moved her tongue to her clit and swirled it around Gina's hardened nerve center.

Gina pressed the back of Crockett's head, forcing her face into her. Crockett could barely breathe, but it didn't matter. All that mattered was making this moment memorable for Gina. Gina was writhing on the bed, encouraging Crockett. Crockett finally sucked Gina's clit between her lips and flicked her tongue over it. Gina cried out as the first orgasm washed over her.

Crockett didn't even wait until Gina had caught her breath. She slid her fingers deep inside her and continued to suck her clit. She felt Gina's insides quiver then clench hard around her as another climax rocked her body.

It took Gina several moments to float back to earth after the orgasm Crockett had given her. She'd been right anyway. Crockett was an exceptional lover. She was half tempted to slip into sleep, completely satisfied, but she wanted to please Crockett the same way she'd pleased her.

She kissed Crockett and tasted herself on her lips. Her flavor was heady. No wonder Crockett had stayed down there so long. Gina kissed down Crockett's chest. She stared at Crockett's small breasts. They were perfect for her lean, long body. She would have looked ridiculous with large breasts. Gina soon tired of staring at them and bent to take one in her mouth. She sucked on it and took half her breast in with it. She sucked hard and played her tongue over the nipple. She noticed Crockett groaning and moving on the bed. She kept at it and soon Crockett let out a low, guttural moan.

Gina released Crockett's breast and looked at her in surprise. "Did that just happen?" she said.

"Yeah. I can come to nipple play."

"That's awesome. Let me have a go at the other one."

She took the other breast in her mouth and she sucked hard again. She rolled the nipple on her tongue and Crockett started to groan again. Finally, she called out as she came.

Gina was pleased with herself. She'd already gotten Crockett off twice and she hadn't even been between her legs yet. She kissed lower down Crockett's taut belly. The feel of her muscles under Gina's lips got her hot all over again. She was finally between her legs and, like Crockett had done with her, took a moment to take in the sight before her. Crockett spread her legs wider and Gina bent to devour her. She lapped all over, inside and out. Gina had Crockett's juices all over her face. She was delicious. Crockett arched off the bed and gyrated, urging Gina to lick and suck everywhere, and Gina was happy to comply. She darted her tongue inside then moved it to Crockett's clit. She sucked and licked, and soon Crockett was calling her name as she rode the waves of her orgasm.

Gina kissed her way back up Crockett's body until she could spoon back against her. Crockett wrapped her arms around her. Gina felt safe and secure there. There was something about Crockett that just felt right. And while she supposed that should have scared her, it didn't. It comforted her.

She fell asleep in Crockett's arms and slept hard until she was awakened in the morning to the feel of Crockett making love to her again. She looked down to see her between her legs.

"What prompted this?" Gina asked.

"You looked too good lying there. I had to have you again."

"I'm not complaining. Help yourself."

Crockett went back to what she was doing and Gina lay back and enjoyed it. Crockett had a magic tongue. She could take Gina places she'd never been before. And then she felt Crockett's fingers slip inside. She tried to maintain her breathing, but she wasn't able to focus on it. She felt all her energy coalescing in her center. It grew tighter and tighter the more Crockett licked and sucked her. And finally, the energy burst forth and shot molten lava throughout her body.

"That was amazing," she said when she'd caught her breath. "Oh my God, you have a talented tongue."

"I'm glad you enjoy it."

"I do indeed. Now, get up here so I can return the favor."

Crockett moved up next to Gina, and once again, Gina kissed her on the mouth before she kissed down her body. She sucked her nipples but didn't spend as much time on them as she had the night before. She wanted to taste her again. She thought Crockett was delicious and couldn't wait to have her again.

She buried her face between Crockett's legs and went to work licking and sucking on every inch she found there. She slipped her fingers inside Crockett while she sucked and licked her clit. She heard Crockett cry out just as she felt her clamp down around her fingers so hard she thought they might break.

"That was a series of really intense orgasms," Crockett said. "Thanks."

"My pleasure."

"So, what do you want to do now?" Crockett said.

Gina's stomach knotted. What would Crockett want to do? Would she want to just leave? Gina didn't like that idea. The idea of spending more time with her definitely sounded good, but she got the feeling that Crockett was a player, and Gina figured she should give her an out if she was ready to get out of there.

"I don't know. What would you like to do?"

"I'd like to take a shower. Would you care to join me?"

"I'd love to."

Gina led the way to her bathroom. She turned on the shower. When the water was warm enough, she stepped in and Crockett walked in behind her. They lathered each other up and then Crockett dropped to her knees in front of Gina. Gina had to place her hands on Crockett's shoulders to brace herself as Crockett took her from another orgasm.

After the shower, they toweled off and got dressed. Gina put on some shorts and a tight T-shirt. Crockett put on her clothes from the previous night.

"So, what now?" Crockett said.

"I don't know. Would you like me to make some coffee?"

"Why don't you let me take you out to breakfast?"

"Are you sure?" Gina was surprised, but pleasantly so.

"Of course I'm sure. Unless you're tired of me already?"

"No way." Gina smiled. "Breakfast sounds wonderful."

LESSONS IN DESIRE

They went to breakfast and Gina had a fantastic time. She and Crockett talked about everything from their childhoods up to their dreams for their futures.

"And what do you plan to do with an advanced degree in English?" Crockett said.

"I guess I want to be just like you." She blushed. "Meaning, I'd like to teach at a university."

"Excellent call. You won't get rich, but you'll certainly love it."

"I don't expect to live lavishly. Though I do plan to supplement my income with writing. I've always wanted to be an author."

"Good for you. I've often wondered if maybe I have a book in me, but I think I'm too lazy. So, I wish you the best of luck."

"Thanks."

"So, what do you want to do after breakfast?" Crockett said. "I mean, do you have plans?"

"No, I don't."

"Would you like to go tubing?"

Gina laughed.

"Seriously? I've heard of it, but I've never gone."

"It's a Chico tradition. And you'll want to go now before all the students are back in town."

"Sounds good."

"Okay. I'll drop you off at your place, then go get some beer and change my clothes. I'll be back at your place in about a half hour. Oh. One thing. Do you have a car?"

"Yes. Why?"

"You need two cars to tube."

"Okay."

"Trust me on this. Now, let's get going."

CHAPTER EIGHT

Crockett dropped Gina off and immediately felt alone. She'd enjoyed her night with her very much and was looking forward to spending the day with her as well. Maybe, if she played her cards right, she'd get to spend the night with her, too.

She stopped by a mini mart and picked up a twelve-pack of beer. She went home and changed into her board shorts and muscle shirt. She checked herself out in the mirror. Not bad. She wondered what Gina would wear. It didn't matter. Gina could rock a burlap sack as far as she was concerned.

She hopped in her truck and drove over to Gina's. She knocked on the door and was pleasantly surprised when Gina opened it. She was wearing short shorts and a bikini top. The outfit really showed off her figure. Crockett wanted her again right then.

"Do I look okay?" Gina asked.

"You look delicious."

"Yeah?" Gina arched an eyebrow.

Crockett didn't try to control herself. She closed the distance between them and kissed Gina hard on her mouth. When the kiss ended, she stepped back.

"Thank you," Gina said. "I don't know what that was for, but I appreciate it."

"Yeah? You're okay if I just randomly kiss you?"

"Of course."

Score, Crockett thought. This might be the beginning of something yet.

"Well, I'd like to do more, but if I do, we'll never get on the river."

"We could always tube another day," Gina said.

Tempting though it was, Crockett was determined to show Gina how nice tubing was.

"We should get going before I change my mind," Crockett said.

"Fine. If you insist." Gina grinned at her.

Crockett took her hand and led her out to the parking lot.

"You follow me. We'll park my car at the washout. Then we'll get tubes and take your car up to the takeoff area."

"Okay. I'll meet you there."

Crockett drove through town, careful to keep her eye on Gina to make sure she didn't lose her. When they hit Sacramento Avenue, there was very little traffic and even less on River Road.

Crockett pulled into the washout and parked among the vehicles already there. She climbed into Gina's car and gave her directions to Scotty's, where they would get their tubes. The tubes fit in Gina's car much better than they did Crockett's truck.

They arrived at the landing and Crockett carried her tubes and the ice chest and Gina carried her tube. They got the beer situated, then Crockett sat in her tube and pushed off. She watched as Gina did the same, then she paddled over so she could hold Gina's hand for the trip.

They drank beer and relaxed in the sun. Well, Crockett relaxed as much as she could for being so close to Gina dressed as skimpily as she was. Her full breasts were barely contained by her bikini top and Crockett wanted to take the top off with her teeth. But she tried to focus on other things as they floated.

"Isn't this fun?" she asked.

"It's very relaxing. I'm enjoying myself immensely."

"Good."

The float was over too soon for Crockett's liking, but she still hoped to get to spend more time with Gina. They got out of the water at the washout.

"What an awesome way to spend a Sunday," Gina said.

"Yeah? You really enjoyed it?"

"I did indeed. Thank you for that."

"My pleasure. Now let's go return the tubes and get your car."

Crockett was sad when she dropped Gina off at her car. She didn't want to be away from her. What was wrong with her?

"You can follow me back to your place," Crockett said. "Then I'll head over to mine."

"Will I see you again?" Gina said.

"Sure. Dinner tonight?"

"That would be wonderful."

"Great. I'll pick you up at six."

Crockett's heart soared as she drove back to town. Gina wanted to see her again. She couldn't wipe the smile off her face. Nor did she want to. She got home and showered and dressed in some gray cargo shorts with a purple golf shirt. She knew the shirt brought out her eyes and she wanted to look good for Gina. She wondered if she'd get to spend the night with her again. She could only hope at that point. She'd have to see how dinner went.

At five forty-five, she left her house and drove to Gina's apartment. She was a few minutes early and hoped Gina wouldn't mind. When Gina opened the door, she was wearing another calf length cotton sundress. This one was dark green and really showed off her features.

"You look amazing," Crockett said.

"Come in."

Crockett stepped inside and, as soon as the door was closed, kissed Gina on the cheek.

"I mean it. You look great."

"You look awfully fine yourself."

"Thank you."

"Would you like a beer?" Gina said.

"I'd love one."

"Great. Go ahead and have a seat on the couch. I'll be right there."

Crockett sat on the couch, and memories of the previous night washed over her. She remembered the kisses they'd shared and it fanned the fire already burning in her core.

Gina arrived with the beer and a glass of wine for herself.

"I really like your apartment," Crockett said.

"Thanks.

"I didn't really take the time to look around last night, you know?"

"I appreciate that."

Crockett laughed. She liked Gina's honesty. It was one of her best traits. One of many. She could write a laundry list of what she liked about Gina. And she had a feeling the list would grow the more she got to know her.

She took a drink of her beer and pondered what to say next.

"Do you like Basque food?" she said.

"I don't know that I've ever had it."

"Hm. Well, I hope you will because I'm taking you to one of my favorite restaurants tonight. And it's Basque."

"Well, I'm up for new things, so it sounds good to me."

"Excellent."

Gina sat sipping her wine wishing Crockett would kiss her again. She tried to think of something, anything, to say, but all she wanted was to kiss Crockett. She took another sip of wine, then set her glass down.

"Everything okay?" Crockett said.

"Kiss me."

"What?"

"Kiss me. Please."

"Gladly."

Crockett set her beer down and kissed Gina passionately. Their tongues danced together for what seemed an eternity. When the kiss finally ended, they were both breathless. Gina picked up her glass of wine.

"Thank you," she said. "I needed that."

Crockett picked up her beer.

"You never need to ask me twice to kiss you. I'm always up for that."

"I like the sound of that."

They finished their drinks and went out to Crockett's truck to drive to the restaurant. The restaurant was on the north end of town. It smelled delicious when they walked through the door. There were unfamiliar scents to Gina, but they smelled wonderful.

"I think I'm going to like it here," she said.

"Great. I'll put our name in and we can go wait in the bar."

Gina sat at a table in the bar while Crockett went to order their drinks. She liked the restaurant. It felt homey. She watched Crockett walking back from the bar carrying their drinks and had to smile. Crockett was gorgeous, and for the second night in a row, she was on a date with Gina. Gina was happy.

Crockett handed Gina her wine then sat down beside her.

"What's the smile for?" she said.

"No reason. Just loving life."

"Good. I was kind of hoping I might be the reason for the smile, though."

"You definitely are, Crockett. You definitely are."

Gina surprised herself at her honesty with Crockett. She wasn't playing hard to get at all. She normally dated for a while before she slept with a woman, but Crockett was different. There was an animal magnetism between them, but there was something else. Something deeper. She hoped Crockett felt it, too.

They were called to their table and Crockett stood until Gina was seated. Then she sat and looked deep into Gina's eyes. Crockett's eyes were dark blue—a color Gina had come to associate with desire.

"What's up?" Gina said.

"Nothing. Just admiring the view."

"You say the sweetest things."

"I mean them."

"Thank you."

"You're welcome."

"So now let's admire the menu, shall we?" Gina said.

She looked over the menu. It all looked so good. And expensive. She was glad this was on Crockett. There was no way she'd be able to pay for a meal at a place like this. Sure, she had money from her job in Illinois, but she was hoping not to have to get a job in Chico. But if she did, she did. For now, though, money was tight.

"I don't know if I can decide," she said.

"I know. It's all good. I'm getting the rib eye, but I don't know if you're much of a meat eater."

"I am, but that chicken with shrimp looks really good."

"Okay. So get it."

"If that's okay with you."

"Babe, whatever you get is okay with me."

Gina didn't miss the term of endearment. She fought to keep her smile from taking up her whole face. She gave Crockett a small grin.

"Okay, then that's what I want."

The waitress came and they ordered.

Almost as soon as the waitress disappeared, food started showing up. There was soup, spaghettini, and salad. And that didn't count the Basque style beans, red potatoes, and green beans that were served with their meals. Gina could hardly eat any of her chicken. She managed to finish her shrimp, but that was it.

"I'm going to have to take my chicken home," she said. "I'm stuffed."

"No problem. I'm sure it'll be good heated up tomorrow. Speaking of tomorrow, what are you doing all day?"

"I don't know. I'll probably hang out by the pool for a while and work on my tan."

"I love your tan," Crockett said in a hushed tone.

"Thank you. And I think I'll hit the bookstore and get books for my classes."

"Good idea. Better to get them now than to wait too long and not get them."

"Right. Plus, there's a better chance of getting used books if I go early."

"Good point."

"And what's your day look like?" Gina asked.

"Teaching. What else? And grading papers. Same ol' same ol'."

"Would you like to come over for dinner after work tomorrow?" The words were out before she had time to think about what she was asking. She was sure Crockett was going to start pulling away any minute now.

"I'd like that. You mean to tell me you can cook, too? Or will we be having leftover chicken?" She laughed.

Gina laughed as well.

"No. I make a mean lasagna. It'll knock your socks off."

"What about the rest of my clothes?"

"Hopefully, it'll knock them off, too."

Crockett took a sip of beer.

"I like the way you think, Gina."

"Thanks. I hope I'm not coming on too strong."

"Not at all. I love it."

"Good."

They left the restaurant and walked out to Crockett's truck.

"It's a beautiful evening," Gina said.

"It is. I love Chico in the summer."

"Have you always known this would be your home?"

"I always hoped. I came here as a freshman and fell in love with the town and the campus and dreamed someday I'd make it my home."

"And you did. You're lucky."

"Maybe someday you'll make it your home, too."

"I can only hope."

They drove back to Gina's apartment. In the truck, Gina took Crockett's hand in hers. She wondered what Crockett's reaction would be, but Crockett just smiled and didn't say a word. When they arrived at Gina's apartment, Gina looked over at Crockett.

"Would you like to come in for a beer or something?"

"Or something?" Crockett arched an eyebrow.

"Read into it what you want," Gina said as she slid out of the truck.

Crockett exited on her side and came around to take Gina's hand.

"You sure are open about holding my hand," Gina said. "I'd heard Chico was a pretty conservative town."

"Not so much around the campus area. But if you get out to the agricultural areas, yeah, they're more conservative."

"Oh, good."

"Why?" Crockett said. "Do you like it when I hold your hand?"

"Of course I do."

"Excellent."

They entered Gina's apartment and Gina went to the kitchen to get a beer for Crockett and some wine for herself. She walked into the living room and was taken aback by Crockett sitting there. She wasn't doing anything, just looking at Gina, but Gina paused, unable to believe how good-looking Crockett was. And she was with her. It blew her mind again that Crockett would choose her over the myriad other women she knew she could have. But for the moment, she had chosen Gina and Gina was going to enjoy every second she had with her.

"You okay?" Crockett said.

"Yep. I'm fine."

"Okay. Good."

Gina handed Crockett her beer. Their fingers touched during the handoff, and Gina felt shockwaves flow through her. Electricity flowed where her blood should. And yet she didn't pull away. She stood there, enjoying the sensation for a moment before Crockett took her beer from her.

Gina sat next to her on the couch. She sipped her wine. She loved the feeling of being so close to Crockett. She could feel her warmth radiating off her. She wanted her again and sincerely hoped Crockett was on the same page. She seemed to be, but she could always be just teasing. That would be painful. Gina needed Crockett. She needed her touch, her taste. She wanted to make love with her right then.

Patience, she told herself. Patience. It'll happen in due time. All in due time.

"What are you thinking about?" Crockett asked.

"Nothing," Gina lied. "What about you?"

"Just how nice it is being here with you."

"It's very nice, isn't it?"

"It is. Now, I'm going to be bold and ask if I can spend the night again."

"I was hoping you'd want to."

"Are you kidding? I'm dying to."

"Me, too," Gina said. "I mean I'm dying to share my bed with you again."

"Excellent."

Crockett leaned in and kissed Gina. It was soft and sensual at first, but soon grew into something deeper and more powerful. She ended the kiss and Gina's head was spinning. She was lightheaded with desire. She tried to make the room stop circling around her. She took a sip of her wine.

"Wow," she said. "That was some kiss."

"Yeah it was."

"You're a really good kisser, Crockett."

"I think we kiss well together."

"That's true. We really do."

"Let's finish our drinks," Crockett said. "I have big plans for you."

Molten heat coursed through Gina. She knew what Crockett's plans were and couldn't wait to get started.

CHAPTER NINE

Crockett's desire for Gina burned deep. Her need was an all-consuming ache. The degree to which she had to have Gina was powerful, to the point that she could think of nothing else. She stood and took Gina's hand. She helped her off the couch and kissed her again. Her legs shook, her whole body trembled. This was so new to her, but she liked it. She liked it a lot.

They walked to Gina's bedroom where Crockett again undressed Gina, admiring her in her nakedness. She was such a beauty to behold. Crockett couldn't get enough. She quickly undressed and pulled Gina against her. The feel of their skin against each other sent electricity coursing through her anew. She thought she would burst from the heat searing her insides.

Crockett eased Gina onto the bed. She climbed up and lay next to her, never taking her gaze from her body.

"You're beautiful," Crockett said. "I know I say that a lot, but I mean it. You're gorgeous."

"Thank you. You're quite a specimen yourself."

Gina pulled Crockett in for a kiss. It was a long, languid kiss that left Crockett wanting more. Crockett broke the kiss and kissed down Gina's body. She stopped to play with her breasts and suck her nipples in her mouth. She played over them with her tongue until they were hard nubs. She released them then and kissed lower. She nibbled and sucked on Gina's belly until Gina placed her hand on Crockett's head and urged her lower.

Crockett was happy to oblige. She settled between Gina's legs and took a moment to admire her. But a moment was all she could take. She had to taste her again. She bent her head and took Gina in her mouth. She sucked her lips and ran her tongue between them. She plunged her tongue inside her. She swirled it around and hit all Gina's sensitive spots. Then she slipped her fingers in and placed her mouth over Gina's clit. She sucked hard on it, and soon Gina was crying her name as she came. Crockett kept doing what she was doing and coaxed several more orgasms out of Gina. Finally, she kissed up Gina's body until she was lying next to her again.

"You are amazing," Gina said. "You sure know how to please a lady."

"Your body was made for pleasing."

"Well, it's yours to please any time you like."

Hearing that Gina appreciated her was great and all, but Crockett was in serious need of release. If Gina didn't make love to her, she was going to have to excuse herself and take matters in to her own hands.

But Gina wasn't going to leave her hanging, as she soon discovered. Gina sucked on Crockett's nipples while she rubbed her clit. The combination was overwhelming for Crockett, and soon she was crying out as a strong wave of an orgasm crashed over her.

"I love how sensitive your nipples are," Gina said when she'd finished.

"I love how you make them feel."

"Good. I hope to make them feel like that a lot."

"Me, too."

Crockett wrapped her arms around Gina and fell into a sound sleep. She awoke in the morning a little confused about where she was. Then the memories came back to her. She wanted to take Gina again, but she looked at the clock instead. Shit! She had to get home to get ready for work. It would be cutting it close trying to get to work on time. She eased herself out of bed and started getting dressed.

"You sneaking out of here?" Gina asked quietly.

"No. I mean I guess I am. But I just didn't want to wake you. And I've got to go get ready for school."

"Oh, yeah."

"We still on for tonight?"

"Of course."

"Great." Crockett kissed her. "I'll see you then."

Crockett walked out into the early morning air with a spring in her step. She drove to her house and took a shower and dressed for school. Her attire was pretty much the same to teach as it was to go clubbing. Except, instead of golf shirts, she wore button-down shirts. She slipped on some deck shoes and drove to campus. Her day started with office hours. She was sitting in her office when Melinda came in.

"Hey, Crockett. How are you?"

"I'm great. How are you?"

"How was your date with my TA?"

"Gina. Her name is Gina. And it went great. It turned into a weekend together."

"Oh really?" Melinda arched an eyebrow.

"Yeah. She's really something else."

"She's something else? Are you falling for her?"

Crockett shrugged.

"I don't know. Maybe."

"Crockett, she's a grad student in your department. I hardly think it's appropriate for you to be involved with her."

"She's not my TA. Nor is she in any of my classes that I know of. There's nothing inappropriate."

"I don't know," Melinda said. "Something just doesn't feel right."

"And see? That's where you're wrong. Something definitely feels right here."

"Well, I guess I hope for your sake it works out."

"Gee, thanks."

"No. I mean, I'm happy for you. You look really happy. I've never seen you looking like this before. But I can't help but wonder what happens if your paths cross here on campus."

"If that happens, which I'm sure it won't, but if it does, we'll deal with it."

"How?"

"I don't know and I don't want to think about it right now."

"Fair enough."

"You guys want to get together Friday night?" Crockett asked. "Dinner and dancing?"

"I don't know if that would be a good idea…"

"She's your TA. It's not like you're sleeping with her. And if you're refusing to try to discourage me, it isn't going to work. I think it would be a good chance for you two to get to know each other. After all, I got to know Terry."

"This is different."

"Not really. And we've had drinks with our TAs before."

"Yeah. I suppose we have."

"Good. So it's settled. We'll meet you at seven at Crush for dinner."

Gina woke up several hours after Crockett had left. She lay in bed remembering the night before. It had been wonderful. Crockett was so good in bed. And she was as much fun to please as she was to be pleased by. Gina could make love to her all night long.

She finally dragged herself out of bed and into the kitchen where she made coffee. She was missing Crockett more than she thought she would. They'd only spent a day together, but it had been so right. She sure hoped Crockett was feeling this, too. Otherwise she'd be in big trouble. She didn't know how to find out how Crockett was feeling without asking her point-blank. And she didn't know if she was brave enough to do that.

She drank her coffee and contemplated her day. It was still early, so she had one more cup of coffee then changed into her swimsuit. She went to the pool. There was no one around, so she took her favorite lounge chair and lay out for an hour. It was starting to get hot, so she jumped in the pool and swam a few laps. She got out and lay in the sun some more until she was dry. Then she went inside and took a shower and got ready to head to campus.

Gina put on shorts and a T-shirt and drove to the student union, armed with her list of books she would need for Melinda's class. She bought them all and then headed to the grocery store to buy ingredients for her grandmother's lasagna recipe. She picked up a bottle of wine, as well as some beer for Crockett.

She went home to start making the sauce. It would take the rest of the day to simmer to perfection. She wondered what time Crockett would be over. They hadn't decided on any time. She hoped it would be early, because she missed her. But then again, she hoped she'd at least have time to put the lasagna together before she got there.

The sauce was simmering, so Gina took out one of the books for Melinda's class and started reading it. She was so lost in it she jumped when her phone rang.

"Hello?" she said.

"Hey, babe."

"Hi, Crockett. What's up?" Gina looked at the clock. It was already four thirty.

"I just wondered what time you wanted me to come over."

"What time are you through teaching?"

"I'm through now."

"Why don't you come over at five? That'll give me time to get the lasagna in the oven."

"Sounds good. I'll see you then."

Gina closed the book she was reading and set about making the lasagna. When it was all put together, she put it in the oven. She opened the bottle of wine and sat down to wait for another five minutes. She'd barely sat down when there was a knock on the door. She opened it to see Crockett looking handsome as usual.

"Come on in," Gina said and stepped away from the door.

"You look delicious," Crockett said.

"In this outfit?" she laughed.

"Yes, in that outfit."

Crockett closed the distance between them and kissed Gina lightly on the lips.

"What was that for?" Gina said.

"I thought you said I could kiss you whenever I wanted."

"I did say that."

"And I wanted," Crockett said. "So I did. By the way, it smells delicious in here."

"Thanks. I hope you'll like it. It's my grandma's recipe."

"Ah yes. With a last name like Moreno I guess I'd expect good Italian food."

"Exactly. I bought some beer, too. Would you like one?"

"That would be great."

"Have a seat. I'll be right out."

Gina's heart raced as she went to the kitchen to get the beer and wine. Crockett had kissed her for no reason. Did Crockett like her as much as she liked Crockett? She wished she could ask. She wished she could figure out how to broach the subject. But she didn't want to muck up what they had right then. She reminded herself it had only been going on since Saturday night. Who even knew what they had?

She carried the drinks into the living room and sat next to Crockett on the couch. Even a few inches away from her she could feel the heat radiating from her. She felt the desire in the air between them. And the longing inside her made her want to forget the lasagna. She wanted to take Crockett to bed right then.

"So how was your day?" Gina asked.

"It was good. We're all so ready for summer session to end, you know? Students and faculty alike."

"I bet. But then the real work starts."

"I don't know. Sure, semesters are longer, but summer session you cram so much into such a shorter period of time. I think I prefer semesters. Do you have your schedule yet?"

"Yep. That's how I knew I would be TAing for Melinda."

"Good. I hope my name isn't on that list of instructors you have."

"Nope."

"That's good news," Crockett said.

"Yeah, that might have been awkward."

"To say the least."

They sipped their drinks until the kitchen buzzer went off.

"Ah," Gina said. "Dinner's ready."

"Most excellent. I'm starving."

"Would you like beer with dinner or wine?"

"I think I'd like a glass of wine, please."

"Coming right up."

Gina went to the kitchen and took the lasagna out of the oven. She set it out to cool then poured two glasses of wine and took them to the table. She set the table for dinner and went back to the living room.

"The lasagna has to cool for a few minutes. We wouldn't want to burn our mouths."

"No. Especially since I have plans for our mouths later."

"Oh you do, do you?"

"Well, I thought I did. Isn't that okay? I mean, are we thinking the same way here?"

"Yes, we are. I'm only teasing you. Believe me, we're both thinking the same thing."

"Well, that's a relief."

"Okay. I think we can eat now," Gina said.

She led Crockett to the dining table in her kitchen and had her sit down while she served them. The lasagna smelled amazing to her. She only hoped Crockett would like it, too.

"Oh my God, that smells good," Crockett said. "My mouth is watering."

"Good. Enjoy."

Crockett raised her wine glass.

"To new beginnings," she said.

What did she mean, Gina wondered. Was she referring to Gina just moving to Chico? Or to the new semester? Or to them? She knew she should ask but couldn't find her nerve. She simply raised her glass and clinked it against Crockett's.

"To new beginnings," she said.

Crockett winked at her and her stomach did a somersault.

They each took a bite of their lasagna.

"This is delicious," Crockett said. "I mean it's really, really good."

"Thank you. I love to cook."

"Well, you can cook for me anytime you like."

"I'd like that."

"So would I."

They ate the rest of their dinner in silence that wasn't strained, but wasn't comfortable either. Gina kept replaying everything Crockett had ever said to her. She was sure she was into Gina. Or else she wouldn't be there, right? She was lost in her thoughts when Crockett interrupted them.

"That was delicious," she said. "Are you through?"

"I am."

"Great." She stood and took the plates to the sink.

"That's not necessary," Gina said.

"Maybe it's not necessary but it's what I want to do. You cooked, so I'll clean. You can busy yourself by putting the leftover lasagna away. Oh, and I have a question for you. Do you have any Tupperware or anything like that?"

"Sure. Why?"

"I'd really like to take some lasagna for my lunch tomorrow. I mean, if that's okay."

"That's fine." Gina smiled inside. Crockett really did enjoy her dinner. Gina wanted to burst out in the biggest grin ever, but she played it cool. "I'm glad you liked it."

"I did."

Crockett finished loading the dishwasher while Gina put some lasagna in a container for Crockett's lunch. She put it with the rest of the leftovers in the refrigerator. Crockett moved up behind her and wrapped her arms around her. She nuzzled the back of Gina's neck. Gina felt her nipples harden at the contact.

She turned in Crockett's arms and wrapped her own around Crockett's neck. She kissed her lightly, simply enjoying the contact of Crockett's lips against her own. The feeling was amazing.

Crockett ran her tongue along Gina's lips, and Gina opened her mouth, welcoming her in. She loved the way Crockett's tongue danced so easily with hers. It incited the flame scorching her insides. They kissed like that for a while; Gina wasn't sure how long. When the kiss ended, she was weak in the knees.

"Come on," Crockett said. She took Gina's hand and led her down the hall. Gina quickly stepped out of her clothes and lay down. She watched lasciviously as Crockett stripped. Her mouth watered as she watched each inch of flesh become exposed. Her palms itched to touch Crockett again.

A naked Crockett lay next to Gina and Gina ran her hand all over Crockett. She rested her hand between her legs. Crockett gently grabbed her by her wrist.

"Oh no, you don't. You relax. I'll love on you first."

"But I want you."

"And you shall have me. But first, relax and let me please you."

Gina lay back and let Crockett have her way with her. Crockett teased and pleased her breasts and sucked her nipples until Gina couldn't stand it any longer.

"Please, Crockett. Please."

Crockett looked at her and smiled.

"If you insist," she said. She kissed lower and finally rested between Gina's legs. "I don't even know where to start."

Crockett ran her fingers over the length of Gina. She finally slipped them inside her and rubbed as deep as she could reach. Gina felt full. Crockett knew just what to do. Gina moved all over, making sure Crockett hit all her special spots inside.

Crockett lowered her mouth and licked Gina's clit and Gina soared into the abyss. She floated back to earth to find Crockett still loving her. Her fingers continued to move in and out while she continued to lick and suck Gina's clit. Gina came several more times until she didn't think she could take any more.

She lay there catching her breath while Crockett kissed her way back up her body.

"You are so amazing," Crockett whispered in her ear.

"No. You're the one who's amazing. Now lay back and let me at you."

Crockett lay on her back and spread her legs. Gina slid her hand between her legs again. She found Crockett wet and ready for her. She plunged her fingers deep inside her while she sucked on Crockett's nipples.

"More," Crockett said. "I need more."

Gina slipped another finger inside and continued to move them in and out. She focused her tongue on Crockett's nipples. She reached her thumb out and ran it over Crockett's swollen clit causing Crockett to cry out.

Gina backed into Crockett's arms and fell into a deep sleep.

CHAPTER TEN

Crockett woke early the next morning and thought about sneaking out without waking Gina, but she remembered how Gina had reacted the day before so thought better of it. She kissed her on her forehead.

"Hey, babe?" she said.

"Hm?"

"I'm taking off now, okay?"

Gina pushed herself up on an elbow.

"Okay. Thanks for waking me up to say good-bye."

"You know, I was thinking."

"About?"

"Maybe I should bring some clothes over here so I don't have to get up and leave so early. I could shower and get dressed and leave from here."

Crockett held her breath. She knew what she was proposing could terrify Gina. Hell, it scared her half to death. But she wanted to do that. She wanted to have extra clothes at Gina's house. She wanted to be able to make love to Gina in the morning before she had to shower and leave. Why was Gina taking so long to answer?

"That sounds good," Gina finally said.

"Yeah? You sure?"

"I'm positive. That way you don't have to leave in the middle of the night."

Crockett laughed.

"It's not the middle of the night. But it is earlier than I like to get up."

"Do you want me to make some coffee?"

"No thanks, babe. You go back to sleep. I'm going to grab the lasagna and hit the road."

She kissed Gina on the lips and left.

Crockett was walking back to her office after teaching a class. She ran into Melinda in the hall.

"Hey," Melinda said. "You want to go grab some lunch? I'm starving."

"Thanks, but Gina made lasagna for dinner last night so I've got leftovers."

"You had dinner with her last night?"

"That I did."

"Crockett, is this really serious?"

"I don't know. I'm not sure what she's feeling, but I could certainly get serious with her."

Melinda followed Crockett into her office and sat down, but she didn't say anything.

"What?" Crockett said.

"I'm worried," Melinda said.

"So you've said. Look, we're both adults and we seem to like each other. I think we know what we're doing and I think it's safe."

"I really would hate to see you hurt."

"If she hurts me, she hurts me. I'm willing to take that chance right now."

"You know all this time I've teased you about settling down, I never dreamed it would be with a student."

"Why not? She's smart, funny, sexy as hell. She's perfect for me."

"I'm glad you think so. I just hope she's on the same page as you."

"I think she is. Sorry about not wanting to get lunch. I'll walk with you, though."

"No thanks. I think I need to be alone."

"Come on, Melinda. Be happy for me."

"I'm trying. I really am."

"Okay. Well, we're still on for Friday, right?"

"Right."

"Good."

Crockett ate her lunch and graded papers until it was time to go over to Gina's. She hadn't asked if she could come over. So she went home and packed a duffel bag with spare clothes. When her bag was packed, she called Gina.

"Hello?"

"Hey, babe, what are you doing?"

"Nothing. Just reading."

"Sounds good to me. You want some company?"

"Sure," Gina said. "That would be great. But I didn't make any dinner tonight."

"That's okay. I'll take you out."

"Are you sure?"

"I'm positive. I like spoiling you."

There was silence on the other end of the line. Had she said too much?

"Well, I won't argue about that."

"Good. I can be there in about fifteen minutes. Is that okay?"

"Yeah. That sounds great. I'll be ready for you."

"Excellent. And, babe? I'm bringing over some extra clothes. You still okay with that?"

"Yeah. I'm fine with it."

"Phew. Okay. I'll see you in a few."

Crockett put her phone in her pocket and grabbed her keys. She drove over to Gina's apartment. Gina opened the door wearing another sun dress. She looked fantastic.

"Wow. You in those sundresses drives me crazy. Maybe we should skip dinner and go straight for dessert."

"You're such a dog," Gina smiled. "I'm hungry, though."

"Fair enough. So am I. How do you feel about seafood?"

"I love it."

"Great. We'll go to Pelican's Roost."

"I'll have to trust you. Although, thanks to you, I'm learning my way around town."

"Good. Oh, I forgot to mention, we're going to dinner and dancing Friday night with Melinda and her girlfriend. Is that okay with you?"

"Sure. It'll be nice to get to know her better."

"I thought so, too."

"I hope she won't mind. I mean, I'm her TA and all. I feel comfortable, but will she?"

"I'm sure she'll be fine." Crockett hoped she sounded convincing.

"You don't sound so sure."

"Oh," Crockett said. "I'm sure she'll be okay with dinner. I just hope she'll be okay with us."

"Us?"

Crockett's stomach tightened. Oh, shit. She'd said too much. How could she back track? No, she thought, she should just bite the bullet and go for it.

"Us, meaning you and I seeing each other. I mean, we are seeing each other, aren't we?"

Gina stood quietly for a moment. Crockett wanted to leave. If she'd made a huge mistake, she was afraid her heart might actually break.

"At the very least we're seeing each other," Gina finally said.

"Phew. I thought so."

Gina laughed. It seemed to ease the tension somewhat.

"You're so silly," Gina said. "You know I like you."

"Yeah? And I like you."

"Good. Now, about dinner?"

"Oh yeah, come on, let's go. I'm starving."

They enjoyed their dinner in quiet conversation. Crockett was so excited that Gina had pretty much agreed that she was her girl.

She wanted to shout it to everyone around her. She knew she'd look like an idiot, but she almost didn't care. Almost.

After dinner, they went back to Gina's apartment and Crockett took Gina back to her bedroom. Crockett undressed Gina and lay her back on the bed. She quickly stripped out of her own clothes and lay with Gina. Gina was so soft against her. She knew she wouldn't be able to just lie there enjoying the feeling. She had to have Gina.

Crockett kneaded and loved on Gina's breasts. She sucked on first one nipple and then the other. When they were as big as she could make them, she continued to pull them deep into her mouth and run her tongue over them. She skimmed her hand down Gina's silky stomach to where her legs met. The feeling of the moist air radiating from her center made Crockett's own clit swell. She slid her hand over Gina's slick clit before moving her fingers deep inside her.

She plunged her fingers deep inside, then twisted her hand as she took them out before repeating. Gina was bucking on the bed, meeting every thrust. She was breathing heavily and Crockett knew she was close. She took her hand out and rubbed her clit with everything she had. Gina held Crockett close while she came.

Crockett loved her again and again, bringing her to more and more orgasms. When she was satisfied that Gina had had enough, Crockett moved up next to her and held her close. She was aroused beyond words but knew Gina needed to recover before she would get her turn.

Gina lay in a state of bliss. Crockett had loved her so well. But then she always did. But she knew she couldn't lie like that for long. Crockett and her awesome body lay next to her and she needed to claim her. She needed to own her. She needed to love her.

She rolled over and looked Crockett deep in her eyes. They were dark with passion.

"Are you ready for me?" Gina whispered.

"Beyond."

Gina kissed Crockett's chest until she came to her breasts. She sucked a nipple deep in her mouth and ran her tongue over the tip. Crockett squirmed. Gina kept at it until Crockett moaned during her release.

Gina slid her hand between Crockett's legs. She was drenched. Gina smiled knowing it was all her who made her feel this way. She teased Crockett with her fingers, dragging them over every inch of her. She played them over her clit briefly and moved them in then out of her.

Crockett grabbed Gina's wrist.

"Please," she said. "Please focus."

Gina laughed.

"Okay. I'll take care of you."

She ran her fingers around Crockett's clit before pressing into it and rubbing it just how Crockett liked. Crockett cried out her name as the orgasm cascaded over her.

Gina fell asleep with Crockett's arms around her. She woke up in the middle of the night and snuggled closer to Crockett. She felt safe and cared for. And she liked it. She fell back asleep smiling from ear to ear.

She was having an erotic dream. She was lying on the bottom of the ocean and was surrounded by mermaids. The mermaids were taking turns making love to her. She was writhing as they took her to one orgasm after another. Two held her legs open and the others took their turns between them.

She woke up to find Crockett positioned between her legs. She was licking and sucking, and in no time Gina called out her name as she reached a mind blowing orgasm.

"Good morning to me," Gina said.

"Mm. And me."

Crockett kissed up Gina's body until she could kiss her on the mouth, sharing the taste of her orgasm with her.

"You taste so good," Crockett said.

"And now let's see how you taste."

Gina moved down to where Crockett's legs met. She gazed longingly at what she saw. She loved how beautiful Crockett was.

She loved how she smelled, how she tasted. She buried her face in Crockett's glory. She licked over every inch and sucked every millimeter. She left no part untouched and was rewarded when Crockett arched off the bed, called her name, and collapsed.

"Wow," Crockett said. "That was something else."

"Yeah, it was. To what do I owe this morning's pleasure?"

"Ah. That was because I have clothes here so don't have to get up and sneak out in the middle of the night." She smiled. "So we have more time for fun in the morning."

"I like the sound of that," Gina said. She liked Crockett having spare clothes at her house. She liked that Crockett considered them seeing each other, but somehow she wanted more. She wanted to know it was more than simply seeing each other. She wanted them to be an item. She supposed it didn't need to be said out loud. They were an item. She knew it in her heart.

"I should hit the shower," Crockett said.

"You do that. I'll get the coffee going."

She heard the shower start and started the coffee. She tried to be strong, but she wasn't. She walked into the bathroom and climbed into the shower with Crockett. The shower was small and they were pressed together.

"Well, hello," Crockett said.

"I need a shower too, so I thought why waste water?"

"Exactly."

Crockett lathered Gina up all over, paying special attention to the area between her legs. She rinsed her off then got on her knees to please her. Gina's knees went weak and she had to dig her fingertips into Crockett's shoulders to keep from falling over.

They got out of the shower and dried off. They kept their towels wrapped around them as they sat at the kitchen table and drank their coffee.

"This is nice," Gina said.

"Yeah, it is. But someday I'd like to have you over to my place. I'm sure Archie would love you."

"Who's Archie?"

"My cat. I'm sure he wonders where I've been lately."

"Okay. We'll spend some time over there. I don't mind at all."

"Maybe tonight?"

Gina laughed.

"You just brought your clothes over and now you want to stay at your place?"

"I just really want you to see it. And meet Archie."

"Okay, so tonight you'll pick me up and we'll go over there?"

"Or, I could give you my key and you could go hang out there and wait for me to get home. I'm usually home by five."

"I could make dinner over there if you'd like."

"That would be great."

"Okay, we'll plan on it. What would you like?"

"Surprise me."

"Will do," Gina said. She took Crockett's key and entered her address in her phone. She kissed Crockett good-bye and watched her walk to her truck. She was such a fine specimen of womanhood. And she was all Gina's. At least, that's how Gina saw it.

Gina hung out at her apartment reading one of the books she needed for Melinda's class. At two o'clock, she left to go to the grocery store and then to Crockett's. She arrived at Crockett's armed with ingredients for scampi. Even though they'd had seafood the night before Gina had decided to make scampi. She had an excellent recipe and knew Crockett would love it.

She let herself in and was greeted by a huge orange cat who rubbed against her legs.

"Well, hello," Gina said. "You must be Archie."

Archie meowed at her. Gina pet him. Then she set about making dinner. She had all the prep work done when Crockett came home.

"You look so good in my house," she said. "So natural."

"I feel pretty natural. Since you're home I'll go ahead and start dinner. Why don't you grab a beer and pour me a glass of chardonnay?"

"You got it."

The kitchen was very large for such a small house. Crockett's house was more of a cottage, but it was quaint and clean and Gina loved it. She sipped her wine while she prepared dinner. She served up and they sat at the dining room table.

"I love your house," Gina said as they started eating.

"It's not much, but it's mine."

"And Archie is a love."

"That he is," Crockett said. "This is delicious."

"I'm glad you like it. I was a little worried about having seafood two nights in a row, but figured you probably wouldn't mind."

"Not at all."

"Good."

They ate all the scampi, and when dinner was over Crockett washed the dishes.

"We've got a good thing going, don't we?" Crockett said.

"That we do."

"Now, we could watch television or something. Or we could go to bed."

"You know when I'm around you bed is just about all I can think of," Gina said.

"Is that right?"

"Yes, it is."

Gina moved close to Crockett. Crockett rested her hands on Gina's hips. Gina laced her fingers behind Crockett's neck.

"So, bed it is then." Crockett pulled Gina to her and kissed her. It was a kiss Gina felt everywhere in her body. She broke the kiss to come up for air.

"Oh, my," she said. "That was a nice appetizer."

"Just wait until you see the main course."

"I can't wait."

Crockett took Gina's hand and led her to her bedroom.

"Tell me something, Gina," Crockett said. "Do you ever use toys?"

Gina's heart fluttered. Toys? They always added a certain something to the experience.

"What kind of toys are we talking about? I like them. I think they're fun. What kind do you have?"

"I have a wide variety."

"Let's see them."

Crockett went to her dresser and opened her top drawer.

"Come take a look."

"Oh my God. That's quite a selection you have. Are they all clean?

"Of course," Crockett said. "They've all been through the dishwasher."

"Okay. This one looks fun." Gina pulled one out of the drawer.

"Ah yes. The butterfly kiss. It massages your G-spot and clit at the same time. And these rings tease your lips. You want to try it?"

The toy sounded like heaven to Gina. She couldn't wait to try it.

"Yes, I do. I can't wait."

Gina quickly undressed and lay on the bed spread-eagle for Crockett to do what she wanted with her. Crockett peeled off her own clothes and kissed Gina hard on the mouth. Their tongues danced together, and it was driving Gina mad with desire.

Crockett moved her mouth to Gina's breasts. As usual, she sucked one nipple and then the other deep into her mouth. While she sucked, she turned the toy on and pressed it inside Gina. Gina felt full from the toy. She liked the feel of the toy tickling her clit and teasing her lips. Crockett withdrew the toy then slid it back in. She did this a couple more times before Gina grabbed her wrist.

"No," Gina said. "Hold it deep inside me and tight against me."

Crockett did as she was instructed while she continued to suck on one of Gina's large nipples.

Gina rocked against the toy and soon lost all coherent thoughts. The only thing that mattered was the toy inside her and on her. She focused only on it as she rode it. She closed her eyes and saw lights explode as more orgasms than she'd ever experienced at one time racked her body.

"Holy shit," she said when she could speak. "That was amazing."

"Excellent," Crockett said. "I'm so glad you enjoyed it."

"We need to get one of those for my place, too."

"Consider it done."

When Gina could breathe normally again and Crockett had slid the toy out of her, she kissed Crockett hard on the mouth. She lay on top of her and continued to kiss her. She kissed her cheek down to her earlobe. She slid lower and kissed her breasts before taking a nipple deep in her mouth. Crockett tangled her fingers in Gina's hair as Gina suckled her. Crockett's breathing became shallow until she cried out. Gina moved to the other breast and did the same thing until she brought Crockett to another climax.

She climbed between Crockett's legs where she took Crockett over the edge several more times.

"Okay, babe," Crockett said. "That's enough."

"Are you sure?"

"I'm positive. But thank you. I'm worn out."

"If you say so."

"I do."

Gina climbed up into Crockett's arms and fell asleep.

CHAPTER ELEVEN

Friday arrived and Crockett and Gina slept late. They had spent Thursday night at Gina's again so they could hang out around the pool all day. Crockett loved the easy routine they had fallen into and had to remind herself it had only been going on for a few days. It seemed like they'd been together forever. And she was happy, so very happy. Happier than she'd ever been in her life. She'd had no idea this type of happiness could actually exist.

Once they were both awake, Crockett pleased Gina in a way she'd never pleased another woman. The connection was so deep, so intense. It was profound, rooted in something she didn't quite understand. But whatever it was, Gina reacted to it with equal fervor. She was so responsive to everything Crockett did. It only turned Crockett on more.

And then Gina would love her. Again, the depth of feelings was new and unusual, but oh so welcome. Gina took her to places she'd never been before. And she'd come for a lot of women throughout her life, but none affected her the way Gina did.

When their lovemaking had ended, Crockett climbed out of bed.

"I'm famished. What do we have to eat?"

"I have some eggs, but nothing to go with them. There's still leftover lasagna, but I don't know about that for breakfast," Gina said.

"Leftover lasagna sounds wonderful. I want a huge piece. I mean it. I'm starving."

"Great. Let's eat and have some coffee. Then we can hit the pool."

They ate and drank their coffee and Crockett just kept watching Gina, unable to believe they were really an item. It had all happened so easily. She considered herself the luckiest woman on earth.

"What?" Gina said.

"What what?"

"You're staring at me."

"I'm sorry. You're just so beautiful. It's hard not to stare," Crockett said.

"Oh, please."

"I mean it."

"Well, thank you."

"So, tell me, are you going to wear a bikini to the pool today?"

"Would you like me to?" Gina said.

"Very much so."

"Then I will. As long as you like it."

"Well, I've never seen you in an actual bikini. I've seen you in shorts and a bikini top, but not in bikini bottoms. I'm looking forward to the sight."

"I hope it doesn't disappoint," Gina said.

"I'm sure it won't. Your body is smokin' hot. Come on. Let's go put our suits on. I'm ready to hit the pool."

They changed into their suits, and it was all Crockett could do not to peel Gina's suit off and have her way with her.

"You're staring again," Gina said.

"I'm sorry. I want to get you out of that suit and back into bed."

"Well, then let's do that. We don't have anything to do until seven. Let's go back to bed."

Crockett didn't need to be told twice. She unhooked the top of Gina's bikini and watched her breasts fall free. She knelt down and peeled her bottoms off with her teeth. She was so close to Gina's center. She could smell heaven. She knelt upright and ran her tongue over Gina who moaned in pleasure.

She eased Gina back on the bed without breaking contact with her. She continued to lick and suck her until Gina pressed the back of Crockett's head into herself. She fought for her breath but continued her ministrations until Gina froze then collapsed on the bed.

"Okay," Crockett said. "I think I can go to the pool and maintain myself for a while now."

"What about you?"

"Oh, I'm fine. I just had to have you. You can have me later."

"If you're sure," Gina said.

"I'm positive."

They went out to the pool to find it somewhat crowded.

"Everyone must have taken the day off," Gina said.

"I guess. Or else they're all in summer session or teach it." She glanced around the area for anyone she might recognize. She saw no one.

"There are a couple of lounges together over there." Gina pointed.

They walked over and got comfortable.

"Damn, it's hot today," Crockett said.

"It's hot every day for those of us not lucky enough to be in air conditioned offices."

"I suppose that's true."

They lay in the sun for a while until Crockett pleaded heat stroke and jumped in the water. Gina sat on the edge of the pool and dangled her legs. Crockett pulled herself up on her arms and hovered just next to Gina.

"I like the view from here," Crockett said quietly.

"You're so bad." Gina smiled.

"Just being honest."

They climbed out of the pool and dried off, then got back in when it got too hot. After they'd been out for a few hours, Gina pleaded hunger.

"I need lunch," she said.

"Sounds good to me."

They walked back to the apartment hand in hand.

"I have sandwich makings," Gina said.

"A sandwich would be great. Do you need some help?"

"No. You sit at the table. I'll make the sandwiches."

Crockett sat and watched Gina's flowing movements in the kitchen. She was so easy on the eyes. And she was all Crockett's.

"Hey," Crockett said. "You're still not nervous about tonight are you?"

"No. Well, maybe a little."

"You don't have to be, you know. You'll be with me. That's really all that matters."

"True. But I don't want to do anything to make Melinda not want me as a TA."

"I highly doubt you could."

"Still," Gina said. "I worry."

"Well, please don't."

"I'll try."

She served their lunches and Crockett grabbed a beer to go with hers. They enjoyed their meal, and after they'd put the dishes in the dishwasher, Crockett pulled Gina to her again.

"And now," she said. "It's time for dessert."

"It is?" Gina arched an eyebrow at her.

"Yes, it is."

Crockett kissed Gina hard on her mouth and pressed her against the kitchen counter. She pulled down her bikini bottoms and fingered her until she collapsed against her.

"You're incorrigible," Gina said.

"You're too beautiful to pass up."

Gina stepped all the way out of her bikini bottoms and took her top off.

"Oh my God," Crockett said.

Gina led the way down the hall knowing Crockett would follow her. She needed more and also wanted Crockett. She planned to make both those things happen in her bedroom. When they got to her room, Crockett ran her hands all over Gina's bare skin leaving a trail of gooseflesh everywhere she touched.

"Take me," Gina said. "Take me again."

"I will. Don't worry about that."

Gina lay on the bed and watched Crockett take off her outfit. She stood there, looking firm and fantastic. Gina lay back to let Crockett have her, knowing it wouldn't be long before she got to have Crockett as well.

Crockett loved her with a ferocity that showed her need. She had her fingers deep inside Gina while she sucked on her clit. Gina felt every bit of her being coalesce in her center. There was nothing but Crockett and the power of energy deep inside. Crockett hit the spot just right and the energy shot forth throughout her body as one after another climax washed over her.

When she had floated back to her body, she took her turn loving Crockett. She loved her deliberately and purposefully. She sucked her nipples, which she knew Crockett loved, while she played her fingers over the wetness between her legs. In no time, Crockett cried out and hugged Gina close as she rode her orgasm.

They napped then and at five-thirty got out of bed to get ready for dinner. They took a shower together where Crockett made Gina come several more times. Finally clean, they dressed and sat down to have a drink before they headed to the restaurant. Gina hoped the glass of wine would help calm her nerves. The closer the time came to actually having dinner with Melinda got, the more the butterflies fluttered in her stomach.

Crockett reached out and grabbed Gina's hand.

"You okay?" she said.

Gina took a deep breath.

"I will be."

"Please don't stress, babe."

"I'm trying not to."

"Look. Melinda is my best friend. Tonight is about my best friend and my girl meeting each other. It's got nothing to do with you being her TA, okay?"

Her girl? Gina was certain that's what Crockett had said. The nerves were replaced with a joy she'd never known.

"Your girl, huh?" Gina said.

"Well, sure. I mean, you are my girl aren't you?"

"Yes," Gina said, smiling wide. "I am."

"Good."

Crockett kissed her then. It was a light kiss, but it conveyed so much. Gina found herself more relaxed by the moment. Until it was time to leave. They set their drinks down and stood. Crockett took Gina's hand and gave it a little squeeze. Gina squeezed hers back hard.

"Easy," Crockett said. "It's just dinner with my friends."

"Okay."

"Okay?"

Gina nodded.

"Good."

They walked into the restaurant and Melinda and a woman with short gray hair waved to them.

"That's them. Come on," Crockett said.

She placed her hand on the small of Gina's back and guided her toward Melinda and the other woman. When they reached the table, Crockett made introductions.

"Melinda, you remember Gina?"

Melinda smiled.

"It's so nice to see you again."

"You too."

"And," Crockett said, "this is Melinda's girlfriend, Terry."

Terry stood and offered Gina her hand. Gina took it.

"It's nice to meet you, Terry."

"Nice to meet you, too."

Terry sat back down and Gina and Crockett did the same. Under the table, Crockett rested her hand on Gina's thigh. The feeling of her warm hand comforted Gina more than words could. She told herself to relax and have a good time.

"So, what brings you to Chico?" Terry said.

"It has a good program for English."

"And what do you plan to do with an advanced degree in English?" Melinda said.

"I'd love to teach. And I think Chico State would be a great place to do that."

"Well, we love it there, don't we, Crockett?" Melinda said.

"We do indeed."

"But why Chico?" Terry asked.

"It sounded like it had a nice small town feel about it, and I didn't want to go to some conglomerate type college where you're a nameless, faceless number. I wanted a small, intimate setting. Chico seemed perfect."

"Well I, for one, am glad you chose it." Crockett squeezed her knee.

"Thanks." Gina smiled at her.

"So you two have really hit it off, huh?" Melinda said.

"We have," Crockett said. "It's weird, but it's real."

"Weird?" Gina said. "Yeah. I suppose it is. But it's definitely real."

"I'm just glad we found each other," Crockett said.

"Me, too."

"Well, if you're happy then we're happy for you," Melinda said. She raised her glass of wine. Crockett raised her beer, Gina raised her wine, and Terry raised hers. "To new relationships."

"Hear, hear," they all replied and took drinks. Gina was starting to relax. She was with friends of Crockett, just like Crockett had said. It wasn't scary. And Melinda seemed okay with her. So, as long as she didn't do anything to make an ass out of herself, the evening should flow smoothly, she thought.

Their dinner arrived and they ate in animated conversation. There was talk of where everyone had grown up and what had brought them all to Chico. They talked about the old days when Chico was known as a party town and how much it had calmed down over the years. Gina listened to it all and jumped in when appropriate. She was very relaxed by the end of dinner.

"You ready for some dancing?" Crockett asked the group.

"We are," Melinda said.

"Great. Then let's go."

They walked out into the warm night air and stood by their vehicles.

"Okay," Crockett said. "We'll meet you there."

"Sounds good."

Crockett and Gina got in the truck.

"How bad was it?" Crockett asked.

"It wasn't bad at all. As a matter of fact, I had a really good time."

"Good, because if I have my way we'll be spending lots of time with them."

"Sounds good to me."

They pulled into the parking lot of The Montrose right next to Terry and Melinda. The four of them walked in together. The music was already blaring. Gina was in the mood to dance. It was early so there were plenty of seats available. They found one down by the dance floor. Three of them sat down while Crockett went to get the first round of drinks. Gina sat there chair dancing while Terry took Melinda out on the floor. Crockett came back with the drinks to find Gina all alone.

"They left you alone?" she said.

"Yeah. I don't blame them. When the music calls, you have to dance."

"True. Are you ready to dance now?"

"I am."

They walked out on to the floor and took their place next to Terry and Melinda. The four of them danced to one song after another. Eventually, they were all thirsty and made their way back to their table.

Gina sipped her chocolate martini and replayed the evening in her mind. It felt good to be out with Crockett and her friends. Sure, staying home with Crockett had its definite advantages, but once in a while it would be fun to go out as a group. And it was nice being at the club where they could hold hands or she could enjoy Crockett's arm around her without worrying. She hoped they would all get together again soon.

The night wore on and Terry and Melinda finally pleaded tiredness. They said their good nights. Crockett looked at Gina.

"How're you doing?" she said. "You ready to head home?"

"I am."

"Great. Where to?"

"It doesn't matter to me."

"Okay, we'll go to my place tonight."

"Sounds good," Gina said.

Once they were inside Crockett's house, Gina was in her arms. She felt like a teenager the way she was kissing all over Crockett. But she couldn't get enough. She needed more. And she knew Crockett would deliver.

They kissed together as they went to Crockett's room. They fell on the bed together. Gina loved the feel of Crockett's weight on her. It felt so real, so right.

"I need to get you out of those clothes," Crockett said.

Gina stood and took her dress off, but Crockett gently grabbed her wrist before she could take off her bra and panties.

"No," Crockett said. "I want to take those off."

She unhooked Gina's bra and caught her breasts as they fell free. She played with them, rubbing her thumbs over her nipples, urging them harder. Then, she peeled Gina's panties off.

"Oh yeah," Crockett said. "That's how I like to see you."

Gina lay there exposed to Crockett and felt more aroused by the minute.

"Get naked," she said. "Come to bed with me."

Crockett undressed, but instead of climbing into bed, she stood there looking at Gina.

"What?" Gina said. "Why aren't you in bed with me?"

"Just a second," Crockett said. She turned to her dresser and Gina knew what was coming. It was the butterfly kiss again. She almost squealed in delight.

"Oh yes, Crockett. Please. I'm so ready."

"Are you though?" Crockett stared at Gina between her legs. "Oh yes, you are. You are swollen and wet, and oh my, I can only imagine how good this is going to feel."

She slid the toy into position then slowly plunged it inside so all the parts lined up. She withdrew it a little then pushed it back in. She repeated this several times until Gina grabbed hold of the toy and pressed it against her. She gyrated on it and bucked against it and finally all the spots hit at the same time and Gina had the most powerful orgasm she'd ever have from a toy.

"Oh my God," Gina said. "Oh my God."

When she finally opened her eyes, Crockett was smiling down at her.

"That good, huh?"

"Oh yeah. Better."

"Well, good. I'm glad you enjoy it."

"You said something earlier," Gina said. "You said you could only imagine how good the toy was going to feel. Does that mean you've never used it?"

"That's right," Crockett said. She hoped she didn't have to try to guess all the women she had used it on.

"Well, tonight is your turn, then."

"Oh I don't know about that. I'm kind of the butch, you know?"

"You're all butch. Don't worry. I've noticed. But it won't make you less of a butch for just trying out a toy."

"I don't know…"

"Please, Crockett. I'll never tell another living soul about it."

"You swear?"

"I swear."

"Okay then."

Crockett lay naked on the bed with her legs spread. Gina bent to taste her. She ran her tongue over her briefly before lining up the toy. She slipped the toy inside and Crockett gasped.

"Holy Jesus, that feels good," Crockett said.

"Doesn't it?"

Crockett did the same thing Gina had done. She took the toy away from Gina and used it on herself, making sure every spot was hit. She finally screamed Gina's name as she came again and again.

Crockett finally put the toy on top of the dresser and climbed back into bed to hold Gina.

"So you'll honestly never tell anyone you saw me use a toy on myself?" Crockett said.

"I promise."

"Good. Because I may just want to use it again."

"It's a lot of fun, isn't it?"

"It is."

"I like the personal contact more," Gina said. "But once in a while, that toy is a major treat."

"I agree. Now let's get some sleep. Tomorrow we've got a butterfly kiss to contend with again."

CHAPTER TWELVE

Saturday morning, they picked up where they'd left off Friday night. Crockett got up and scrubbed the butterfly kiss then used it again on Gina bringing her to one earth-shattering orgasm after another. Seeing Gina so turned on did nothing to cool the fire burning in her own belly. When Gina had had enough, Crockett rolled over and opened her legs. Gina took the toy but Crockett held her wrist.

"No. No toy. I want you."

Gina seemed happy to oblige. She slid between Crockett's legs and licked and sucked on every inch of her. In no time, Crockett was crying Gina's name as the orgasms rolled over her.

After, they lay there together and Crockett lazily dragged her hand up and down Gina's back. She felt so good, so right.

"So, what do you want to do today?" Crockett said.

"I want to go tubing again. If that's okay."

"That's beyond okay. I love tubing."

"Great. Then get your outfit on and we'll have to stop by my place to get my suit and my car."

"My things are at your place, babe. So, yeah, we'll have to go there first."

"Oh yeah. I forgot about that."

They drove over to Gina's and Gina started to undress to put on her shorts and bikini top. She didn't get that far. Crockett was on her as soon as her top was off.

"We're never going to make it to the river, Crockett," Gina said.

"We'll get there eventually. I just need you. Like, right now."

She peeled Gina's shorts off and laid her on the bed. She kissed her passionately while she slid her hand between her legs. She used her fingers to work their magic and made Gina climax several more times.

"Okay, hot shot," Gina said. "Your turn."

"No. I'm fine."

"How can you be fine? Doesn't making love to me turn you on?"

"You know it does. But sometimes I can be okay. Other times I need you to take me immediately. This is one of those times that I'll be okay until later. Trust me."

"Okay. If you insist."

"I do. Now let's get dressed so we can get going."

"That's what I was trying to do," Gina said.

"I'd say I'm sorry, but I'm so not."

Gina laughed.

"You are so bad."

"But that's how you like me."

"It is indeed."

They spent the afternoon on the river and afterward stopped by a burger joint on the river to eat some lunch. They were relaxed and happy when they drove back to town. They had agreed to meet at Gina's apartment. Crockett pulled in just ahead of Gina and parked in what they had dubbed her parking place.

She got out of her truck and walked over to Gina.

"You want to get in the pool?" Crockett said. "It's still pretty damned hot."

"Sure. Go on over. I'll meet you there."

"I can't go. I don't have the key, remember?"

"Oh yeah. You don't live here, do you?"

"No," Crockett laughed. "It only seems like I do."

"No. You live in that totally cute house over on East Sixth."

"That I do. With Archie the cat."

"Who's the greatest cat ever," Gina said.

"I'd have to agree with that."

"Okay. Come on. Let me put my bottoms on and we'll hit the pool. You, my friend, will sit at the kitchen table while I change."

Crockett feigned a pout.

"That won't work on me," Gina laughed.

Crockett laughed as well and sat at the kitchen table while Gina changed. When Gina came out in her bikini, Crockett let out a low wolf whistle.

"Damn but you're gorgeous."

"Thank you. So are you. Now close your gaping mouth and come on."

The pool area was crowded, but they were able to find a couple of lounge chairs. Crockett threw her towel on one and then jumped in the water to cool off. The temperature was easily one hundred degrees and she felt like she was melting.

Gina jumped in, too, and surfaced looking more stunning than ever with her hair slicked back and rivulets of water cascading over her breasts.

"You look amazing," Crockett said.

"So do you."

"No. I mean...I don't even know how to describe how excited you have me right now."

"Really?"

"Really."

"Well, cool your jets, cowgirl. You'll need your energy for the ride you'll be taking a little later."

Crockett loved the sound of that. She wished desperately that everyone would leave the pool and leave Gina and her alone so she could show her just how turned on she was. But that wasn't going to happen, so she just relaxed in the cool water and tried to think of something else.

"So have you bought your books for all your other classes yet? Or just Melinda's?" she said.

"So far just Melinda's. I really need to buy the rest of them."

"How's your schedule look?"

"Pretty manageable, I think."

"Good. I'm glad to hear that."

They spent the next hour in the water staying cool.

"You ready to go in before we become prunes?" Gina said.

"Sure."

They laid out in the sun to dry off then headed into Gina's apartment to cool off.

"You ready for a shower?" Crockett said.

"Of course."

Just like their previous showers, this one included generous lovemaking and Gina held tight to Crockett at the end.

"My legs are shaking so badly I can't stand on my own," she said.

"Good."

Crockett helped Gina out of the shower and to her room. She eased her down onto the bed so she could gain her strength.

"That was something else," Gina said.

"I'm glad you enjoyed it."

"That's an understatement. Now get up on this bed now."

Crockett wished she was strong enough to say no, but she needed Gina's touch too desperately. She lay next to her and got comfortable. Gina started by sucking her nipples to make her come, then moved lower. She kissed and licked and sucked between Crockett's legs until Crockett cried out again.

They lay together for a while after, catching their breath.

"So are we going out tonight?" Gina finally said.

"Sure. Dinner and dancing?"

"Well, I could probably go to the store and get something to make dinner."

"Nonsense. I love taking you out. We'll go somewhere fun."

"Okay, but not too fancy, okay?"

"Sounds good. You like Mexican?"

"I love it."

"Do you like margaritas?"

"Ooh. They're dangerous, but I love them."

"Well, tonight you can stick to them. We'll have them with dinner and then you can continue with them at The Montrose. No chocolate martinis tonight, okay?"

"Sounds fair."

"Good."

Gina ran her hand over Crockett's body, feeling a stirring deep within her. No, she told herself. Not again. Not now. She could wait until later. She didn't want Crockett thinking she was some wanton hussy. Although, she probably already did. She propped herself up on an elbow and looked down at Crockett.

"What's up?" Crockett said.

"You know I'm not like this with everyone."

"Huh? Like what?"

"Like fall into bed and never get out of it."

"Get out of it? Out of bed? Babe, we get out of bed all the time."

"I know, but you know what I mean. I don't want you to think I make a habit of falling into bed with women I don't know."

Crockett propped herself up on an elbow.

"Babe, where's all this coming from?"

"I don't know. I just feel so sexual with you and I don't want you to think that's how I always am."

"But I love sex with you," Crockett said.

"And I love sex with you," Gina said. She was getting frustrated. Her point was clearly not coming across.

"Sure, we didn't know each other last weekend when we first got together, but I think we can both speak to a connection that was there from the moment we met in Melinda's office. At least I can. And it's turned out to be good and real, and I don't care what you were like with other women. I only care about how you are with me. And I love how you are with me, so don't worry, okay?"

"You're wonderful," Gina said.

"So are you."

Crockett wrapped her arms around Gina and held her tight. Gina relished the feeling until she knew they had to get ready to go.

"It's about time we get dressed," she said.

"Yeah. I suppose it is. You okay now?"

"I'm fine."

"Good."

They dressed and headed out to dinner. Crockett had been right. The restaurant had excellent margaritas and the food was outstanding. After, Gina was almost too full to go dancing.

"Oh my God. I'm stuffed," she said.

"You going to be able to move on the dance floor?"

"I hope so. I may have to sit out the first few dances though."

"And that's okay."

They got to the club and found a table by the dance floor. Crockett went to order them two margaritas and Gina sat by herself at the table.

"Hey, Gina. How are you doing?"

She turned to see Donna standing there.

"I'm doing great. How about you?"

"I'm doing awesome. Hey, how'd your date go the other night?"

"It went great."

Just then, Crockett walked up with their drinks.

"Hi, Donna," Crockett said.

"Hi, Crockett. I was just saying hi to Gina. I'll leave you two alone now."

Gina watched her walk off. Donna turned and gave her a thumbs-up. Gina smiled.

Crockett gave Gina her drink.

"I'm sure these won't be as good as the ones at Tres Hombres, but like I said earlier, I don't think we should mix our alcohol."

"I agree." She took a sip. "Not bad."

The music was playing loud and the beat was starting to move through Gina.

"Let me know when you're ready to dance," Crockett said.

"I'm ready."

"I thought you said you wanted to sit a few out."

"I did, but now that I'm here I want to move."

"Sounds good to me."

They got out on the dance floor and moved for a while until a slow song came on. Gina stepped into Crockett's arms and danced, relishing the feel of Crockett's arms around her. They moved as one on the floor, melded together. Gina was happier than she'd ever been.

The song ended and Crockett whispered in her ear. "You ready to get out of here?"

"So soon?"

"It's up to you."

"Yeah. We can leave," Gina said.

They went back to Crockett's house and made love most of the night. They slept late the next morning. They awoke to Archie standing on the bed meowing for his breakfast.

"His gravity feeder must be empty," Crockett said.

"Or he just wanted to make sure we were alive."

Crockett rolled on top of Gina.

"Oh, I'm very much alive."

She kissed Gina on her mouth before kissing down her body. She finally came to rest between her legs. She slid her fingers inside her while she sucked on her slick clit. Soon Gina felt everything slip away except for the feelings Crockett was creating. She closed her eyes tight and just felt. Crockett was so good at what she did that it didn't take long for bursts of lights to show behind Gina's eyelids as one climax after another tore through her. She finally floated back to earth.

"I can't believe what you do to me," Gina said. "Not get up here. It's your turn."

Gina returned the favor and took Crockett to a very powerful orgasm.

"What shall we do today?" Crockett asked when she had caught her breath. "I mean, besides feeding Archie."

The cat, still on the bed, just stared at them.

"I don't know. What do you want to do?"

"I say we go grocery shopping and stock up your refrigerator,"

"You think so, huh?"

"Sure. You need groceries, and since I eat all the time over there I may as well pay for them."

"I can't allow that," Gina said.

"Why not?"

"It just doesn't feel right."

"It should. It's logical. And I insist."

Gina wasn't sure what to say. She was sure Crockett could afford much more than she could, but she'd already spent so much money on her. Surely an assistant professor didn't make that much money.

"You've already spent so much money on me already," Gina said.

"What have I said about spoiling you? I love to do it. So please let me."

"I can see there's no winning this argument."

"Exactly. Now, let's feed Archie and hit the shower."

"Sounds like a plan to me. I'll go shower while you feed him."

"Huh? You don't want to shower with me?" Crockett's face fell.

"Sure I do. I'm sorry. I don't know what I was thinking."

"You weren't." Crockett laughed. "Give me just a sec to fill his gravity feeder and I'll be ready to go."

Gina watched Crockett as she fed Archie and thought, once again, how lucky she was to have her in her life. She was the perfect woman as far as Gina was concerned. Crockett straightened and looked at her.

"That should keep him for a while. Now, about that shower?"

She took Gina's hand and led her into the bathroom. Their shower consisted of more long, slow lovemaking. They finally rinsed off and got out.

Gina was actually looking forward to going shopping with Crockett. It seemed like such a couple thing to do. And they were a couple. This just solidified it.

"We'll need to stop by my place so I can change," Gina said.

"Sounds good."

Gina changed into shorts and a faded T-shirt and they were ready to go.

"We'll hit the store closest to the campus," Crockett said. "We'll get less looks there."

"Are you really worried about getting looks?" Gina was surprised.

"Who me? No. I was thinking more for you."

"Well, thank you, but I'm fine."

"Great. Still I want to shop there because it's close."

"Sounds good," Gina said.

Gina had never had so much fun grocery shopping. She laughed until she cried as Crockett was inappropriate with zucchinis and other vegetables. The store was fairly empty since it catered mostly to students and the fall term hadn't started. So Crockett seemed to feel free to misbehave as much as she liked.

They got plenty of food for Gina's refrigerator and had planned their meals for the week accordingly. Gina really did feel like she was in a relationship. It was more than just the sex. Clearly. Though that was obviously on Crockett's mind most of the time. She didn't blame her. It was on hers, too.

They went back to the apartment and unloaded the groceries. Then they put on their swimsuits and went out to the pool. It was almost empty, which was nice.

After an hour and a half, Crockett complained of being tired.

"Okay," Gina said. "Let's go take a nap."

"Right on."

They climbed into bed and fell asleep in each other's arms. Gina woke to the feel of Crockett unbuttoning her shorts.

"What do you think you're doing?" she laughed.

"I'm awake. I thought you might want to be, too."

"I am now. Don't let me stop you."

"Great. Now arch those hips and let me get these shorts off you."

Gina complied and lay there, exposed from the waist down. Crockett helped her sit up so she could take her shirt and bra off.

"Now you," Gina said. "You need to get naked, too."

Crockett stood and undressed then lay back down next to Gina. She played with her breasts, kneading her full mounds before twisting and tugging on her nipples. Soon, she replaced her hands with her mouth and moved her hand to the warm, moist heaven between her legs. She played over every bit of Gina until she finally slipped her fingers inside her. She stroked her as deep as she could, taking Gina higher with each touch. Finally, when Gina could stand no more, she reached her own hand between her legs and rubbed her clit. Between the two of them, her world shattered into a million tiny pieces.

When she was back together again, she climbed between Crockett's legs and lapped at all the juices flowing there. She licked as deep inside Crockett as she could before moving her mouth to Crockett's clit. She licked it once, twice, and that was all it took for Crockett to scream as she came.

Chapter Thirteen

Gina enjoyed finals week as Crockett was home earlier than usual every day. They made dinner together every evening and made love every night. She had fallen into an easy routine with Crockett. And she thoroughly enjoyed it. Thursday, Crockett got home later because she'd stayed and graded finals. But when she got home, she was free. She had a week off to do whatever she liked. And Gina knew that included her.

They were eating dinner Thursday night when Crockett broached an interesting subject.

"How would you like to drive down to San Luis Obispo and meet my mom?" she said.

"Your mom?" Gina was shocked. That seemed like a huge step.

"Sure. Why not? She's going to love you. It'll only be for a few days. We can hang out at the beach. I can show you the sights. What do you say?"

"I don't know, Crockett. It's such a big step. I mean, your mom?"

Crockett reached across the table and took Gina's hands in hers.

"My mom is awesome, babe."

"So, she knows about you?"

"It would be kind of hard not to. I mean, I do rather look the part, don't you think?"

Gina had to laugh.

"Yes. You definitely do."

"And my mom would be thrilled if I brought home a nice girl for her to meet."

"She would, would they?"

"Yes indeed. So, what do you say? I'll get Melinda to keep an eye on Archie and we can boogie."

"Shouldn't we let her know first?"

"Sure. I'll call her right now."

She excused herself from the table and made her phone call. Gina took deep breaths. She'd only met one other girlfriend's parents before and that had been a disaster. Of course, they were pretending to just be friends and that was quite a strain. She shook her head. No. This would be different. Crockett's mom would probably be a wonderful person just like she was.

Crockett came back in the room.

"So we're all set. We'll leave tomorrow. It's about a six-hour drive, so we'll have to bring snacks and drinks. Then we'll stay for three days and come back. Oh, Gina. I'm so excited."

Gina smiled, trying to look as excited as Crockett clearly was.

"What's wrong?" Crockett said. "You're still worried?"

"I don't know. Yeah. I guess meeting parents isn't my strong suit."

"Oh really? Is this something you've done a lot of in your life?"

"No. Only once and I crashed and burned."

"Well, you won't this time. I promise."

"I hope you're right. What if Melinda can't take care of Archie?"

"I already called her. She's good to go," Crockett said. "Now let's go buy road trip food."

Gina had to laugh. Crockett's excitement was contagious. Even though she was still nervous, she wasn't as leery at the prospect as she had been. And it would be fun to get away and see some of California.

"What will we see?" she asked as they got in Crockett's truck.

"We'll see the beach and where I went to school and anything else you want to see."

"I mean on the way there."

"Oh, sorry. I was planning on taking I-5, which is pretty much agricultural land, but we can go the route of the Bay Area. It'll take us longer, but at least you'll see some of California."

"That would be great," Gina said. "Will we see the Golden Gate Bridge?"

"Not going down. But we'll spend a day in San Francisco on the way home, okay?"

"That would be wonderful."

They loaded up on chips and soft drinks and Twizzlers and various other forms of junk food. Gina was amazed at all that Crockett was buying.

"We'll never eat all that," she said.

"Oh, you'd be surprised. There's not a lot to do in a car for that long. Besides listen to music, sing your heart out, talk, and eat."

"I suppose you're right. But we're going to gain ten pounds each before we even get there."

"Nonsense. We both have kick ass metabolisms. And you know it."

"Yeah. That's true."

They got home and started packing for the trip.

"What's the weather going to be like?" Gina asked.

"That's hard to say. It depends on the fog situation. I'd pack shorts and T-shirts and bring a sweatshirt, just in case."

"Sounds good to me."

Except, Gina knew she wouldn't be caught dead around Crockett's mom in a T-shirt. She packed shorts and nice, short-sleeved blouses. And a new Chico State hoodie. She was ready.

Crockett packed her duffel bag and soon she was ready to go, too.

"We'll need to swing by my place on the way out of town so I can grab a sweatshirt," she said.

"Sounds good."

"You know what else sounds good?" Crockett leered at Gina.

"Let me guess."

Crockett closed the distance between them and pulled Gina close.

"We may as well get this taken care of now as I doubt you'll want to do this at my mom's house," Crockett said.

"You're right about that."

Crockett kissed Gina softly, tenderly on her lips. The light touches made Gina's head spin. Her heart raced as Crockett's tongue traced her lower lip. She opened her mouth to allow Crockett in. When their tongues met, Gina's world tilted on its axis.

They kissed for what seemed an eternity before Crockett pulled Gina's shirt over her head. She unhooked her bra and caught her breasts as they fell free. Gina loved Crockett's hands on her. She was so gentle and loving. And she turned Gina on no end.

Crockett bent to take one of Gina's nipples in her mouth. Gina moaned with delight. The feeling was pure ecstasy. She fought to maintain her balance as Crockett moved to her other nipple. When Crockett had apparently had enough of her nipples, she stood and kissed Gina again.

Gina's insides were ablaze. She needed Crockett with every ounce of her being. She felt Crockett unbuttoning her shorts and her skin rippled at her touch. Crockett pulled Gina's shorts off and then her underwear. She eased Gina back so she was sitting on the bed. Crockett knelt between her legs and licked the length of her. Gina clenched her teeth and tried not to let go too soon. But it didn't take long. Crockett's tongue was talented and she knew just where to lick and suck. Soon Gina let out a guttural scream as she came again and again.

She lay back on the bed and tried to catch her breath. She hadn't noticed Crockett undressing and only came back to earth to see her climbing onto the bed with her.

"You look wonderful," Gina said. "I love to see you in all your natural glory."

"Thank you."

Gina kissed Crockett and tasted her own orgasms on her tongue. She lazily dragged her tongue around Crockett's mouth before breaking the kiss to nibble down her neck. She moved lower and sucked a nipple in her mouth, taking half of Crockett's breast in her mouth as she did. She moved her tongue over the nipple while she skimmed her hand over her taut stomach. She slid her hand lower and entered Crockett. She slowly slipped her fingers inside then pulled them out. She repeated this several times before Crockett could take no more.

"My clit," she murmured. "Please rub my clit."

Gina was happy to oblige. She rubbed just how she knew Crockett liked it, and soon Crockett arched off the bed, froze, then collapsed in a puddle on the bed.

Gina backed into Crockett and Crockett wrapped her arms around her. Gina fell asleep with a smile on her face.

Crockett woke earlier than usual the next morning. Normally, on her days off she slept late and then woke up to make love to Gina, but there was no time for that that morning. She wanted to get on the road. She was excited about introducing Gina to her mom. She got up and made coffee then went in to wake up Gina.

"Is it time to get up so soon?" Gina said.

"It is, babe. We need to get on the road."

Gina's eyes opened wide.

"Oh yeah. I'd forgotten about that."

"Come on. It's going to be fun. Trust me. Now the coffee's ready so get up and let's have some."

Gina got out of bed and wrapped a robe around her exquisite body, hiding it from Crockett's view. It was probably a good idea because Crockett was weak when it came to Gina's naked body.

And making love to her wasn't an option. They sipped their coffee and washed their cups. They loaded everything in the truck and drove over to Crockett's to get her hoodie. Once that was done, they were on the road.

"I'm so excited," Crockett said.

"I can tell."

"You're going to love my mom."

"So you've said."

"Relax."

"I'm trying."

"Good. So I figure we'll drive for about an hour and then stop for breakfast at Granzella's in Williams."

"Sounds good to me."

"We should be hungry by then don't you think?" Crockett said.

"I think so. I'm starting to wake up now so I think by then I'll be able to contemplate food."

They drove past almond and walnut orchards and rice paddies.

"So this is the scenic route?" Gina said.

"Well, it's all ag until we get to the Bay Area. Then you'll see cities and such. Sorry."

"It's okay. I guess it's important to see all areas of the state."

"Sure. It's home now. You may as well know what surrounds you."

They stopped at Granzella's and each of them ate a hearty breakfast. They walked back to the truck after.

"And you think we're going to need all that snack food?" Gina said.

"Yep. Trust me. Because, except for gas, we're not stopping again until we get to San Luis."

"Yes, ma'am."

They got back on the road. The scenery remained drab until they got to Vacaville, the first city of substance they'd seen since they'd left Chico.

"Do you want to listen to some music?" Crockett said. She handed Gina her phone.

"Sure. What do you want me to play?"

"Choose something off my iTunes."

Gina did and Melissa Etheridge filled the truck.

"Oh yeah. Now you're talkin'," Crockett said.

They sang along with Melissa as they continued their road trip. Finally, they were on the home stretch.

"I can't wait," Crockett said. "I'm so excited."

"When was the last time you were home?" Gina said.

"I don't know. A year or so I suppose. I don't get down here often enough."

"Wow. No wonder you're excited."

"I really am."

They finally came into San Luis Obispo. They came to a stop light and Crockett reached out and took Gina's hand.

"How are you doing?" she said.

"I'm a little nervous, but I'll be okay."

"Good. I'm here with you, babe. Don't ever forget that."

"I won't." Gina smiled weakly at her.

Crockett turned right at the light and they wound their way down a hill in a very nice neighborhood. The yards were well kept, as were the houses. They came to another street and turned right. Crockett stopped halfway down the block and parked in front of a lovely ranch style house.

"You ready?" Crockett said.

"Ready as I'll ever be."

"Okay. Let's go in."

"Will your mom be home now?"

"Sure. She knew we were coming."

"But doesn't she work?" Gina said.

"Mom's retired. I guarantee she's waiting to meet you with bated breath."

"Oh. Okay."

"Come on, babe. I'm with you," she said again.

They walked up to the front door and Crockett knocked. She took Gina's hand and squeezed it. Gina squeezed hers back, a little too hard.

"Relax," Crockett said.

"I'm trying."

Crockett's mom opened the door. She looked good, Crockett thought. Her green eyes brightened at the sight of Crockett standing there.

"Come in. Come in," she said and stood out of the way.

"Hey, Mom," Crockett said and gave her mom a big hug. She felt good in her arms. She'd shrunk a little with age, but she was still sturdy, not frail. She was clearly in good health. She released her and stepped back. "Mom, this is my girlfriend, Gina."

Crockett's mom took Gina into a big hug.

"It's so nice to meet you, Gina," she said.

Gina slid her hands around Crockett's mom and hugged her back. Crockett watched the exchange with pride.

"Gina, this is my mom, Teresa."

"Yes," her mom said. "I'm not Mrs. Devine. Please call me Teresa."

"Okay, Teresa," Gina said.

"Where's David?" Crockett said.

"He's in the office."

"Who's in the office?" a deep voice asked.

Crockett turned to see her older brother standing behind her. She hugged him tight. He was a big man, standing over six foot two and she loved the strength in his arms. She stepped away.

"David, this is my girlfriend, Gina," Crockett said. "Gina, this is my big brother, David."

David extended his hand and Gina shook it.

"Nice to meet you, Gina."

"Nice to meet you, too, David."

"How was your trip?" her mom said. "Come in and tell us all about it. Gina, we have beer, wine, and various other alcohols here. What would you like to drink?"

"I'd love a glass of red wine, please."

"No problem. Crockett, there's beer in the fridge."

"Excellent," Crockett said and made a beeline for the kitchen. She realized she'd forgotten Gina so went back and took her hand. "Come on."

Her mom poured herself and Gina each a glass of wine and sat at the dining room table.

"We can move to the living room if that would be more comfortable," she said.

"Oh no. This is fine," Gina said. She was sitting next to Crockett who had her hand on her leg.

David was still in the kitchen mixing a drink.

"So, how's everything going?" her mom said.

"It's going great," Crockett said with a big smile.

"Clearly. So, how did you two meet?"

Crockett didn't want to tell her mother they'd met at the club. And technically, they hadn't. They'd met in Melinda's office.

"Gina is the TA for one of Melinda's classes this semester," Crockett said. "So we met through her."

"Oh, how nice."

"Yes. I'm really excited about TAing. And Melinda seems like such a nice person," Gina said.

"She's wonderful," her mom said. "She and Crockett have been friends for more years than I can count."

David had finally joined them.

"So you're a student then?" he said.

"I'm a grad student, yes."

"So you've been going to Chico State for a while now and you two just met?"

"Actually, I'm a transfer student."

"Oh. Okay. That makes more sense."

"Yeah, Gina moved to Chico from Illinois."

"Wow," her mom said. "That's quite a road trip."

"Yes," Gina said. "But it was worth it. Or has been so far."

Crockett squeezed her leg under the table.

"How much of California have you seen?" her mom said.

"Just what I saw today." Gina laughed.

"Oh my. Which way did you come?"

"We didn't take I-5," Crockett said. "She wouldn't have seen much of anything if we had. And we're going to spend a day in San Francisco on the way home."

"Now that's a wonderful idea," her mom said. "Are you two hungry at all? We've made reservations at McClintock's in Pismo Beach. I know you two have been on the road all day but it's not that long of a drive to Pismo."

"I think that sounds great," Crockett said. "That way Gina will be able to see the Pacific."

"That would be awesome," Gina said. "I've never seen an ocean before."

Her mom smiled at her.

"Great," she said. "We'll cross one thing off your bucket list for sure."

"And tomorrow, I think we'll spend the day at Avila," Crockett said.

"That'll be fun," David said.

"We have plenty of towels," her mom said.

They finished their drinks and changed their clothes for dinner. Luckily, they'd each brought somewhat nice shirts so they'd be okay at the restaurant.

"Are you sure this is going to be okay?" Gina said.

"Look, we're both wearing shorts, so if it's not okay, we'll be not okay together."

Gina closed the distance between them and kissed Crockett.

"What was that for?" Crockett asked.

"Just for being you."

They drove down by the waterfront so Gina could see the ocean before going to the restaurant, which was situated on a hill. From their seats, they could see the water. Gina was like a little kid. Her excitement was contagious. Crockett couldn't keep the smile off her face.

After dinner, they went home, had some after-dinner drinks, but soon the road trip caught up with Crockett.

"I hate to break up the party, but I'm beat."

"I don't doubt it," David said.

"Your room is all made up for you. There are extra blankets in the closet if you get too cold," her mom said.

Gina and Crockett changed into some oversized T-shirts to wear to bed and held each other. Crockett heard the easy sounds of Gina's sleep, but sleep eluded her. She was too excited about the next few days with Gina.

Chapter Fourteen

The next few days flew by for Gina. She had so much fun touring Crockett's hometown. They had a blast at the beach, though the water was a little too cold for Gina's liking. And Crockett's mom had been the perfect hostess. Gina was sad to see their time there come to a close.

Everyone got hugged as Crockett and Gina said their good-byes. Gina thanked David and Teresa for taking such good care of her and making her feel at home.

"This is your home too," Teresa said. "As long as you're with Crockett, which I'm guessing will be a very long time."

"I sure hope so," Gina said.

"Me, too," Crockett said.

They hugged and stood with their arms around each other.

Finally, it was time to go. Crockett and Gina had stalled long enough.

"If we're going to spend any time in San Francisco, we need to hit the road," Crockett said.

Gina was very excited. She couldn't wait to see what she considered to be the gay mecca. She knew she'd be comfortable there and that she and Crockett would have nothing to fear. Not that she didn't feel safe with Crockett. She knew Crockett would always protect them. But she was looking forward to being out and proud for the whole day.

San Francisco was marvelous. They went to Fisherman's Wharf and Chinatown. They had lunch in Little Italy and got treats in Ghiradelli Square. Finally, Crockett announced it was time to call it a day.

"We need to get going," she said.

"Okay," Gina wasn't too happy to hear it, but knew they still had a long way to go to get to Chico. "I guess we need to get back."

"Yeah, we do. Come on."

Crockett took her hand and they walked back to her truck. Gina couldn't remember the last time she'd walked that much. But it felt good and she'd done it with Crockett which made it special.

The drive back was mellow. They talked about their day, but didn't blare music or anything like that. They ate their munchies and just reminisced about their trip.

"I had so much fun on this trip," Gina said. "Thank you so much for taking me to meet your mom."

"I told you she was awesome, didn't I?"

"You did. Now I don't know what I was so worried about."

"I suppose it's only natural when you're meeting the parents to be a little uptight."

"Yeah, but I feel foolish now. She and David were sweethearts. And they really love you."

"Of course they do," Crockett said. "Doesn't your family love you?"

"Sure. Except for the whole lesbian thing. Dad doesn't get it and Mom says I'm pretty enough to find a nice man."

"Ouch. That's rough."

"Hopefully, when they finally meet you they'll see that I've found someone who makes me very happy."

"I hope so too, babe, because your happiness should be their number one concern."

"You'd think, wouldn't you?"

They finally pulled into Chico and drove through mostly deserted streets to Crockett's house. They'd decided to spend the night there since Crockett had been away from Archie for so long.

Gina was exhausted, but when she stripped to get ready for bed, she felt Crockett's hands on her and was immediately awake. Crockett stroked her whole body lovingly and Gina responded with an animal need. She watched Crockett undress and knew she had to have her.

She ran her hands all over Crockett's firm body before dragging them down to her tight ass. She pulled Crockett against her and rubbed into her, needing, craving more contact.

"Let's get you on the bed," Crockett said. "I've missed you so much. Sleeping with you and not being able to have you these past few days has been torture. I need you now."

Gina wasn't going to complain. She lay on the bed and spread her legs, welcoming Crockett. Crockett climbed between them. Gina could feel Crockett's hot breath on her. She knew what was coming and braced herself for the sheer pleasure of it. Then she felt Crockett's tongue on her and shuddered in anticipation. Crockett covered every inch of her, careful to hit all her favorite spots. In no time, Gina felt her world slip away as Crockett pleased her. Nothing existed except for Crockett's tongue on her. She closed her eyes as Crockett took her closer and closer to the edge. Finally, with one strong stroke of her tongue, Crockett sent Gina soaring into orbit. Bright lights exploded before Gina's eyes as she came several times, each orgasm more powerful than the last.

When she had floated back to earth, Gina kissed Crockett on her mouth before kissing down her body to settle between her legs. She inhaled deeply, savoring Crockett's scent. She dipped her tongue inside her and got dizzy from her heady taste. She licked as deep as she could and lapped at her silky sides. She moved her tongue from there to her clit, where she played over it several times before she heard Crockett scream her name in ecstasy.

They fell asleep and Gina woke in the morning to Crockett sucking on her nipple while she ran her fingers between her legs.

"What are you doing?" Gina smiled.

"Picking up where we left off."

"I do like the sound of that."

"Mm. And I like the feel of this." Crockett wiggled her fingers deep inside Gina.

"So do I."

Crockett continued to play with Gina until Gina could stand it no longer. Crockett plunged in and out of her so Gina reached her own hand between her legs and rubbed her clit. Together, they brought her to several more mighty orgasms.

As soon as she'd recovered, Gina slid her fingers inside Crockett while she sucked on Crockett's nipples. It took no time for Crockett to cry out as she climaxed over and over again.

Crockett soon recovered and lay there holding Gina happily.

"What shall we do today?" she said.

"Hang out by the pool."

"That sounds great. Let's go get breakfast and then head to your place."

Before they left, Crockett loved on Archie, who seemed starved for attention.

"Relax, big guy," Crockett said. "You're fine. You have food and water and lots of love. I'll be back in a couple of days to check on you."

"Maybe we should just hang out here with Archie," Gina said.

"No. He'll be fine."

As if on cue, Archie left the room.

"See?" Crockett said. "He's fine on his own."

They got dressed, went out to breakfast, then went to Gina's to lay out by the pool and relax in the water. There were very few people there that day. Crockett was in the water when she heard her phone ring. She got out and looked at the readout. Professor Bremer.

"Hello?" she answered, wondering what the department chair was doing calling her on break.

"Hello, Crockett? This is Marty Bremer. Do you have a minute?"

"Sure." Crockett sat down. "What's up?"

"Susan Martinez is having problems with her pregnancy. She's in the hospital so won't be returning for this semester. I'm trying to offload her classes. Would you be willing to take on another class?"

Crockett thought about it. Her plate was pretty full. Before she could answer, Marty interrupted her thoughts.

"You would of course be compensated accordingly."

"Sure. I'd be happy to help out. What class are you trying to get rid of?"

"I thought I'd offer you Creative Fiction. It's a Monday, Wednesday, Friday nine a.m. class. Can you do that?"

"I can. I'll take it."

"Can you come over this afternoon and sign a new contract?"

"Sure. I'll be there in an hour."

"Sounds good. I'll see you then."

Crockett got out of the pool.

"What's up?" Gina said.

"I have to get going. They're adding another class to my load this semester, so I need to go sign a new contract."

"Oh, good for you?"

"Yeah. It means more money, and it's not a late in the day class, so I should still be able to get home at a reasonable hour."

"Excellent."

"Are you going to stay here by the pool?"

"I think I am."

"Okay. Can I get your key then? I need to change."

Gina gave Crockett her key and Crockett dried off and put on some nice shorts and a golf shirt. She was ready to see the department chair. She went back to the pool and gave Gina her keys.

"I'll see you in just a little while," Crockett said.

"No worries. I'll be here."

Crockett drove to the university and went to the department chair's office.

Marty stood when Crockett walked in.

"Thank you for doing this, Crockett. I really appreciate it."

"I'm really happy to help out. Honest."

"Great. Here's the addendum to your contract. Take your time and read it over."

Crockett did. It all seemed in order and she would be making an extra chunk of change for her inconvenience. She signed it.

"Okay. That's all we needed. We'll see you Monday."

"Indeed you will," Crockett said.

She smiled as she drove back to see Gina. Life was going so good for her right then. She'd never been happier. She was loving life. She found Gina still at the pool. She called to her and Gina got up, dried off, and walked to the gate.

"You don't have to go in," Crockett said.

"Oh, I think I've had enough tanning for one day."

"Yeah. You don't want to burn."

They walked back to Gina's apartment. Gina undressed.

"I'm going to take a shower," she said.

"Not by yourself."

Crockett stripped quickly and joined Gina in the shower. She loved watching the rivulets of water form on Gina's breasts and then drip off. She took one breast in her hand and bent to lick the water off it. She sucked her nipple until she could feel Gina shaking. She fell to her knees and loved Gina as she knew she liked to be loved. Soon she felt Gina's fingers digging into her shoulders just before she called Crockett's name.

They finished their shower and dried off. They got dressed and Crockett realized she was starving.

"Hey, babe," she said. "Let's grill some steaks tonight."

"I don't have a grill, so we'll have to do it at your place."

"You don't have a grill? That's sacrilege."

"You should have known by now I don't have one. We've never grilled here. It's no big deal."

"Yes, it is. It has to be remedied and immediately. Come on. We're going grill shopping."

"Crockett..."

"Don't 'Crockett' me. You need a grill. Now let's go."

Crockett took her to Home Depot to look at their selection of grills.

"Which one do you like?" she asked.

"They all look the same to me," Gina said.

Crockett laughed.

"Fine. I'll choose one."

"They're so expensive," Gina said.

"We don't need a Cadillac. Just a grill."

Crockett found one for less than one hundred and fifty dollars. She bought it and they took it home to assemble it. Once she had it all put together, she announced it was time to go buy some thick, juicy steaks.

"You are a woman on a mission," Gina said.

"That I am. And while we're out, we'll get some ice cream for dessert."

"Sounds good. I have the makings for a salad, so we will have something besides slabs of meat."

"Excellent."

They went to the local grocery store and Crockett got what she was craving.

"Have you ever had Tillamook ice cream?" she asked Gina.

"Never heard of it."

"You're in for a treat."

They went home and Crockett got the steaks ready and fired up the grill while Gina went about making the salad. They ate their dinner and had dessert.

"This ice cream is delicious," Gina said.

"Good. I knew you'd like it."

"I guess if you like it, I'll like it, huh?"

"Seems that way. And that's a good thing."

"Yes, it is."

"Well, let's get these dishes done," Crockett said. "Because I know something else we both like."

"You do, huh?"

"I sure do."

They finished their dishes and went to the bedroom where Crockett took her time undressing Gina. It was torture for her to go so slowly, but it was a sweet torture. And she knew it drove Gina wild as well.

When she finally had her naked, she laid her on the bed and proceeded to undress herself. She tried to go slowly, but her need was too frantic. She stripped out of her clothes and lay next to Gina, relishing her soft silky skin against her own.

"Your skin is amazing," Crockett said.

"Thank you. It's just my skin."

"It's sleek, like satin to the touch."

"Wow. Really?"

"Really."

Crocket nuzzled her neck and kissed her way down to her breasts. She kissed one, then the other before taking a nipple in her mouth. She skimmed her hand down lower on Gina's body until it came to rest between her legs. She was even softer there, and Crockett wasted no time in entering her. Crockett knew Gina liked it, but Crockett liked it, too. There were so many pliable spots that Crockett could stroke. She loved it. And she knew just where Gina liked to be stroked to give her the greatest pleasure. She took her time and loved Gina until she'd had too many orgasms to count. She'd almost crushed Crockett's fingers with the intensity of them.

When Crockett was sure Gina had had enough, she kissed her on the lips and gently slid her hand out of her. She lay next to her, throbbing with desire. She knew it would take a while for Gina to catch her breath, but she hoped it wouldn't take that long, as she needed her right then.

Gina must have read her mind. She kissed down Crockett's body until she was kneeling between her legs. Crockett felt Gina's tongue on her and moaned. She felt so good. She sucked on Crockett's lips, one of Crockett's favorite sensations. She ran her tongue between them and Crockett arched off the bed. Gina slipped her tongue inside Crockett and Crockett squirmed, feeling the pressure inside her building and knowing she was close.

Crockett felt Gina slide her tongue out of her and knew what was next. She braced herself for it. She felt Gina's lips close over her clit and she felt her tongue brush over it. That was all she needed to get off. She closed her eyes tightly and rode wave after wave of orgasm.

CHAPTER FIFTEEN

S unday night before school started rolled around.

"Are you excited to start graduate school tomorrow?" Crockett asked.

"I am. Are you ready for a new semester?"

"I am. I love the first day of a new semester when I can just hand out the syllabi and let the students leave early. They think I'm great."

"I hope my teachers make us work. My brain needs to be challenged."

"It does, huh? I'm not a brilliant enough conversationalist for you?" Crockett laughed.

"You know what I mean."

"I do. And I'm glad you're looking forward to school starting."

They were finishing up their dinner as they chatted.

"So, babe, I was thinking."

"Yes? And should I be scared?"

"I don't think so. Have I scared you yet?"

"Not really."

"Not really?"

"Well, there was that bit about meeting the mom, but I got over that," Gina said.

Crockett laughed again. Gina was so cute. She loved so much about her.

"Anyway, I was thinking that since tomorrow we both have to go to school, we should probably not spend the night together."

"What? Why not?"

"I just think we both need to get ready so we should be in our own space when we do it. We won't do it every night. Just until we've settled into a routine," Crockett said.

"I think we could work out a routine with both of us here."

"And we'll get there, but I think we should each sleep in our own place tonight. Okay?"

"I don't understand, but if you think it's a good idea, I'll go along with it."

"Great. Now, let's get these dishes done and celebrate the beginning of school before I head home."

They washed and dried the dishes. Crockett took Gina's hand and led her down the hall. She kissed every inch of skin that came into view as she undressed her. As soon as she was naked, she eased her onto the bed and stripped herself. When she was naked, she climbed on the bed with Gina. She left no spot untouched as she kissed all over her body. She paid special attention to Gina's favorite spots and was rewarded when Gina cried out Crockett's name several times.

Gina returned the favor bringing Crockett to multiple orgasms herself. When Crockett had settled down, she held Gina for a long time.

"I don't know if I can sleep without you," Gina said. "I've gotten so used to sleeping in your arms."

"I know. It'll be hard. And maybe after tomorrow, we'll decide we need to just make it work, but I think for our first morning we both need to be fresh."

"Okay."

Crockett got up and started to get dressed.

"So, when will I see you tomorrow? And where?" Gina said.

"I should be done with my day around five. You want me to just come by here after?"

"Yes. That sounds good. Do you really have to go?"

"I really do. Trust me. It's for the best."

"If you say so."

"Good answer," Crockett said.

She drove to her house and walked in to be greeted by Archie demanding attention.

"Hey, buddy," she said. "Let's see if we have any canned food for you. A little treat, maybe?"

She was already missing Gina and it had only been fifteen minutes. She showed Archie all the attention she couldn't show Gina. He ate his food, but soon tired of being petted so he wandered off which left Crockett sitting alone in the dining room.

She got her briefcase to make sure she had syllabi for all her classes. She did. With nothing else to do, she went to bed.

Sleep didn't come easy to Crockett. She'd grown so accustomed to sleeping with her arms around Gina. They felt empty without her. She finally got a pillow out of the hall closet and wrapped her arms around it. She finally fell asleep.

Crockett woke the next day bright and early. She was horny as hell and regretted the decision to spend the night away from Gina. But she really wouldn't have had time to make love to her, which was one of the reasons she'd chosen to go home the previous night.

She showered and dressed in linen slacks, a short-sleeved white button-down shirt, and a black skinny tie. She checked out her reflection in the mirror. Not bad. She'd want to take a class from her. She laughed, grabbed her briefcase, and headed to campus.

Crockett checked into her office. She logged on to her email and printed out the list of students in her first class. Without glancing at it, she put it with her syllabi and went down the hall to Creative Fiction.

She walked into the class and set her things on the podium. Then she looked out at the class. There, sitting in the front row, was Gina. Oh shit, thought Crockett. This can't be happening. She couldn't teach a class with Gina in it. What was she going to do?

It was nine o'clock, so she called the students to order. She was sure her cool façade did little to disguise her shaking voice as she read the roll sheet. Everyone was there.

"My name is Professor Devine," she said. "I'm sure most of you were expecting Professor Martinez, but she's having medical issues that precluded her from teaching this semester, so I'll be taking over this class. I'm a firm believer of easing back into the semester, so today I'll just hand out the syllabus. Wednesday, come prepared to do some real work. You can pick up your syllabus here on your way out. Enjoy your day."

The class was small and everyone picked up their syllabus from Crockett and filed out. Everyone but Gina.

"How did this happen?" Gina asked.

Crockett looked around.

"I'm heading to my office. If you'd like to talk, I'd be happy if you joined me." She tried to sound as professional as she could.

"That would be fine."

They walked in silence to Crockett's office. When they got there, Crockett collapsed in her seat and put her head in her hands.

"Go ahead and close the door," she mumbled.

Gina closed the door.

"How did this happen?" Gina said again.

"When Professor Bremer offered me an extra class, I didn't even think to ask if you were taking it. How stupid of me."

"So how do we fix it?"

"I don't know. I'll talk to Professor Bremer and tell her something came up and I can't teach the class."

"You think that'll work?" Gina said.

"It's going to have to."

"How soon can you talk to her?"

"I'll call and see when she's available."

"Okay. Will you be over tonight?"

Crockett thought about it. She'd have to go over, at least to pick up her things.

"Yeah. We can plan on dinner anyway."

"I don't like this, Crockett."

"Neither do I."

Crockett stood and walked around her desk to where Gina stood. She took her hands and kissed her gently on the lips. Gina ran her tongue along Crockett's lips. Crockett pulled away.

"Oh no you don't."

"I need you, Crockett. I can't go without you."

She kissed Crockett again, and this time Crockett kissed her back, all her frustration and passion being conveyed in that kiss.

Gina sat on Crockett's desk and hiked her skirt around her waist.

"Take me, Crockett."

"I can't."

Gina took Crockett's hand and placed it on her damp panties.

"I need you," she said.

Crockett moved Gina's panties out of the way and entered her. She was only vaguely aware of the sounds of students in the hallway as she took Gina to a powerful climax.

Gina stood and put herself together. Crockett kissed her one more time.

"We'll work something out. Don't worry."

As soon as Gina was out of her office, Crockett called Marty. She got her assistant.

"Hi. This is Professor Devine. It's imperative that I meet with Professor Bremer as soon as possible. When is her earliest available appointment?"

She waited for what seemed an eternity while her assistant checked her schedule.

"She has an appointment at eleven o'clock Thursday."

"Is that the soonest?"

"It is."

"Shoot. I have a class then. Does she have anything that afternoon?" Crockett was feeling desperate. She wouldn't be able to see Gina until this was resolved. Thursday seemed like forever.

"She does. Does three o'clock work for you?"

"That would be great."

"Okay, Professor. You're on her schedule."

"Thank you."

She hung up her phone and sat in her office. She checked her watch. Her next class wasn't until eleven. Until then it was office hours and she didn't have anything to do but worry for the time being.

"Hey you."

Crockett looked up to see Melinda standing in her doorway.

"Hey," she said.

"What's wrong? You look like you've lost your puppy. Are you okay?"

"Professor Bremer needed me to take one of Susan Martinez's classes because she's in the hospital."

"Yeah. I heard about that. So?"

"So, the class I took? Gina's in it."

"Gina? As in my TA? As in your Gina?"

"The very one."

"Crockett you can't keep seeing her."

"Don't you think I know that? And the soonest Professor Bremer can get me in to see her is Thursday afternoon. I'm going to ask to drop the class. I'm sure someone else will pick it up."

"I hope so, Crockett. I sure hope so for your sake."

"Thanks."

❖

Gina left Crockett's office with a pit in her stomach. She knew she couldn't keep seeing Crockett if she was her professor. It could get Crockett in a lot of trouble. She'd just have to trust her to work things out with the department chair. Gina hoped she would be accommodating.

She went to the rest of her classes. Some of them, like Crockett, only gave them a syllabus and sent them on their way, but a couple actually had classes. She was grateful for that as it made her focus on something besides Crockett and her.

When her classes were complete, she walked down the hall to Melinda's office.

"Hi," she said.

Melinda looked up.

"Hello, Gina. What are you doing here?"

"You're my first class tomorrow. I just wanted to make sure I'm ready for it."

"Tomorrow will be easy. Just relax and you'll be fine. Have you read the books for the semester yet?"

"I have."

"Good. Then you're way ahead of the game. Tomorrow, I'll just be handing out the syllabus and getting a feel for the class. I'll introduce you so you'll be front and center from the get go."

"Front and center?" Gina felt panic coming on.

"Not as in solo. Just so the students will know who you are and that they can come to you for help."

"Oh. Okay. That sounds good."

"Trust me. You're going to be fine."

"I do trust you. I've never TA'd before."

"It'll be good practice if you plan on being a professor someday," Melinda said.

"Yes. I suppose it will."

"Hey, and, Gina?" Melinda said as Gina turned to leave. "I talked to Crockett this morning."

Don't cry, Gina told herself. Whatever you do, don't cry now. Not trusting her words, she simply nodded slowly.

"I'm really sorry."

"I just hope she gets out of the class," Gina said.

"I do too."

"Thanks."

Gina left. She pulled her backpack tight on her shoulder and wandered home. She wasn't in any hurry. She still had a couple of hours before Crockett would get to her place. Crockett. She'd

MJ WILLIAMZ

become Gina's whole world in the short time they'd known each other, and she couldn't imagine life without her now.

When she got back to her apartment, she set about making dinner so it would be ready when Crockett got there. Although, why she assumed Crockett would be hungry she didn't know. Gina felt like she had a lead weight in her gut and couldn't imagine eating.

At a little past five, she heard a knock on her door. She opened it to find Crockett standing there, looking gorgeous in her first day of school outfit.

"You look especially hot today," Gina said. "I meant to tell you that earlier."

"Thanks. Something smells good."

"I made dinner."

"Oh, great. Only, I don't know if I should eat here."

"Oh come on, Crockett. It's only dinner."

"Okay. I'll have dinner, but then I'll have to gather my things and head out."

Gina didn't want to cry. She told herself not to, but the tears leaked out of her eyes and trickled down her cheeks. She wiped them away.

"I'm sorry. I don't mean to cry."

"It's okay, Gina. This is hard. Believe me, I get it."

She'd called her Gina instead of babe. Was she already over her? And why didn't she take her in her arms to offer her comfort?

"Did you talk to the department chair?"

"No. Not yet. I'll talk to her Thursday afternoon and we'll get this whole thing straightened out. Just try to be strong, okay? For me?"

Gina nodded. She didn't want to be strong. She wanted to sob while Crockett held her, but that clearly wasn't going to happen.

"Are you ready to eat?" she said.

"Sure."

They sat down and ate their dinner in strained silence.

"So you can't even talk to me?" Gina said.

"I don't know. I just feel awkward even having dinner with you. It's not right until we get everything taken care of."

"I don't see how dinner is a big deal."

"We've been dating for a while. People notice these things. And now that we have a class together, you'd better believe people will be watching us."

"I think you're paranoid," Gina said. "No one cares one bit what we do. I mean, I get that you can't stay here until this whole thing is resolved, but having dinner? Maybe sharing a kiss? That's no big deal."

"No way, Gina. No kiss."

Gina's heart sank.

"Are you serious? This is my apartment. No one is going to know."

"But I will. And you will. And that's what matters. So let me get my things and get out of here."

Gina watched with a heavy heart as Crockett cleared out her drawers and loaded everything into her duffel bag.

"You know," she said. "This isn't easy for me, either."

"It sure seems to be."

"Well, it's not. It's killing me. I can't wait to talk to Professor Bremer."

"I can't wait either. I hope she'll let you teach another class instead."

"Me too. Okay, I should get going."

"Okay. I guess I'll see you in class on Wednesday."

"Yeah. I guess you will. Good-bye, Gina."

"Good-bye, Crockett."

Gina closed the door, sat on the couch, and sobbed.

CHAPTER SIXTEEN

Crockett was a wreck. She hated walking into her class-room and seeing Gina sitting there. Although, thankfully, Gina had taken a seat in the back of the classroom for Wednesday's class. And as Crockett had lectured, she'd made a point not to look at Gina. Because if she did, all concentration was lost. She wanted her so desperately. It was painful.

She managed to get through Wednesday and went over to Melinda's for hot dogs and hamburgers with Terry and Melinda.

"I haven't been able to talk to you," Melinda said. "How are you holding up? And when do you see Marty?"

"I see her tomorrow afternoon. As for holding up, I'm getting by, but that's it. I'm barely surviving at this point."

"That's really horrible, what happened," Terry said. "So you had to teach the class today with her in it?"

"I did. It was so painful. Every time I'd look at her, my heart would skip a beat. I can't wait to have that class dropped from my schedule."

"I sure hope it works out for you, Crockett," Melinda said.

"Thanks."

She drank a few beers and had a hot dog and a hamburger, but as soon as she'd eaten she felt like she was invading their space. She felt like a third wheel.

"I'm going to hit the road now," she said.

"Oh, come on," Melinda said. "It's still early."

"Still. I'd rather go home and wallow in self-pity alone. Thanks for dinner and you guys enjoy the rest of your evening."

"Okay. Let me know if I can do anything to help," Melinda said.

"I will. And thanks."

Thursday morning, Crockett taught her first three classes and then had office hours. She walked down to the café on the creek and bought a sandwich and iced coffee. She took them back to her office. She wished she had some assignments to grade, but she didn't. And no students came by either. She was stuck by herself in her office with her thoughts.

Finally, it was time to go see Marty. She stood, smoothed her slacks, and took a deep breath. She had to do it. And Marty would be okay with it. She had to be.

She walked into the waiting room outside of Marty's office. It seemed like she'd been waiting all afternoon when Marty finally ushered someone out of her office and welcomed Crockett.

"Crockett," she said. "Come on in. What's up?"

"Actually," Crockett took a deep breath. "I wanted to talk to you about my schedule."

Marty arched an eyebrow.

"Your schedule?"

"Yes. I was wondering if I could trade my Creative Fiction class with someone else."

"Trade it? I don't think so. People have planned their semesters, Crockett. Why do you want to trade it?"

"I just don't know if I'm cut out to teach that class."

"What? Why? You've taught it before. And it's your favorite subject besides mythology. So what are you talking about? What's going on?"

"Nothing. I just feel like it's too much. Can you just give the class to someone else?"

"No. It's your class. You signed the contract. Most professors have taken an extra class for Susan. So there's nowhere to put the class. It's yours."

"But, Marty—"

"No. This conversation is over."

Marty stood. Crockett felt like throwing up. She could tell Marty about her relationship with Gina, but no, she really couldn't. Who knew how that would look? She'd have to think of something else. She'd come up with something.

In the meantime, she'd have to continue to stay away from Gina. But she reasoned, she'd have to get with her to let her know how her meeting went with Marty. Although she'd probably cry again and the pain of watching her cry was damned near unbearable.

She called her as soon as she got home. She left her a voicemail asking her to call her back. She changed into her casual clothes and took a beer out of the fridge. She sat down and got comfortable. She figured she might as well be comfortable, since her conversation with Gina was not going to be pleasant.

The more she thought about it, the more she decided she didn't want to have the conversation over the phone. She wanted to talk to Gina in person, so they could go over what other options were available to them.

Crockett was on her third beer when Gina finally called her back.

"How did it go?" she asked.

"Can I come over?" Crockett said, careful to keep her voice neutral.

"Oh? It went that well?" Gina said.

"I just think I should come over."

"Okay. Fine. Whatever. Come on over."

Crockett drove over to Gina's apartment. As she drove, she tried to come up with other solutions to their problem, but couldn't come up with any. She arrived and knocked on the door.

Gina answered it looking amazing in short shorts and a tight T-shirt. Crockett had to slip her hands in her pockets to keep from touching her.

"Well, since you haven't kissed me yet, I can only assume that it didn't go well?" Gina said.

"No," Crockett said. "It didn't go well. I can't get rid of the class."

"So now what?"

"I don't know. I can't come up with any other options."

They stood silently for a moment.

"Do you want to sit down?" Gina finally said.

"I don't know."

"Come on. We can sit at the kitchen table."

Crockett followed her in and sat down. Gina handed her a beer. She took a long pull off it, wishing she could drink something stronger to numb herself. This really couldn't be happening.

"So, if you can't get out of the class," Gina said. "That doesn't mean I can't."

"What?" Crockett looked up at her.

"I mean it. I'll talk to my advisor. He should let me transfer to another class or at least drop that one."

"You'd do that?"

"Crockett, I'd do anything to be with you. This past week has been pure hell and I can't take much more of it. I need us to be together."

"That's an excellent idea," Crockett said. "Why don't you call your advisor first thing in the morning?"

"Believe me, I will."

"Okay. I should get going. I'll see you in class tomorrow."

"Yes, you will."

"Good night, Gina."

"Good night, Crockett."

Gina closed the door behind Crockett and leaned against it. She hoped her advisor would let her transfer classes. She knew she needed the class for her master's, but she could take it a different semester with a different instructor. She just needed not to be a student of Crockett's. That was all there was to it.

She woke up the next morning feeling optimistic about life. She had an easy solution to their problem. It would be quick and painless and they could go back to the way things were. She lay in bed thinking of the way things were and skimmed her hands over her body. She imagined they were Crockett's hands on her, strong and sure. She parted her legs and slid her fingers in between them. She ran her hand over her slick, hardened clit and slipped her fingers inside herself. She moved them in and out, all the while imagining it was Crockett loving her. When she could stand it no longer, she pressed her fingers into her clit and rubbed hard and fast. The lights exploded behind her eyelids as she rode her orgasm.

Feeling much better, Gina got in the shower then got ready for school. She had an hour before her first class, Creative Fiction, so she walked to campus and found a nice quiet bench where she sat to call her advisor. He answered it on the third ring.

"Hello?" he said.

"Hi. This is Gina Moreno. I'm one of the students you advise."

"And what can I do for you, Ms. Moreno?"

"I need to talk to you about my schedule. I'd like to make some changes to it."

"Okay. Hold on while I check my calendar."

There was a silence that stretched on and on.

"I can see you Tuesday morning. Can you be here at eight?"

"Yes, sir. I'll be there."

"Great. I'll see you then."

"Thank you."

She hung up her phone and wanted to sing. She was sure this would all be taken care of Tuesday. Even though Tuesday was a long way off. At least she had her appointment and everything would soon be resolved. She checked her watch. It was time to go to class. The class from hell. The class where she had to spend fifty minutes watching Crockett and trying to concentrate on what she was saying. Oh well, it would be over soon and that gave her something to hold on to.

Gina made it through class and followed Crockett to her office. She stepped inside and closed the door. The close space left little room between Crockett and Gina. She wanted to step up to

Crockett to kiss her and be held by her. But she knew she couldn't do that.

"What's up?" Crockett said.

"I'll see my advisor on Tuesday."

"Not until Tuesday?"

"I'm sorry. It was the earliest he could get me in. I'm really sorry."

"No. Don't be sorry. It's not your fault. And hopefully everything will work out."

"Yeah," Gina said. "But it means one more weekend without you and one more class I have to sit through with you teaching."

"I know. It's hard. But it'll all be resolved on Tuesday. Thanks for doing this."

"I don't know if you realize how important this is to me."

"I think I have a pretty good idea."

"Good," Gina said.

She left Crockett's office and hurried to her next class. She got through the day and was grateful for the weekend. She had a ton of homework to do and was sure she'd be able to stay busy enough not to pout much over the Crockett situation.

Gina started on her homework as soon as she got home. She finished one assignment and settled in to write a short story for Crockett's class. She realized she was hungry, but had nothing to eat at home.

She ordered a pizza then sat back down to work on her story. There were no guidelines for the story. It just had to be between three and five thousand words. She sat there staring at her blank screen. Why couldn't she think of anything to write? It shouldn't be that hard. Then she realized, she would be baring her soul to Crockett in a way she'd never done before. If it was any other professor, she wouldn't have cared as much. But Crockett wasn't just going to grade her, she was going to judge her. So what should she write about?

The doorbell rang and Gina startled. She was still staring at a blank screen. She got up and got her pizza. She ate a piece when the idea hit her. She would write their story, the story of Crockett and herself.

She started typing like crazy. She typed fast and furiously as the words poured out of her. She changed the names and a few things here and there to make it fiction, but it was clearly their story. Only in her version of it, there was a happily ever after. There was no sadness or distress over not getting to see each other even for a moment. In her story, the characters fell in love and lived happily ever after. She sat back and smiled when she finished. She was quite proud of her work. She just hoped it didn't scare Crockett off with all the talk of love and forever in her story. Oh well. She didn't want to change any of it. She thought it was perfect.

She helped herself to another piece of pizza and checked her clock. It was after one in the morning. And she was barely tired. She was too amped from writing. But she knew she had to get some sleep. She put the pizza away and climbed into bed.

Sleep didn't come right away. She tossed and turned, playing out every scenario that could happen the following Tuesday. She truly hoped things would go their way. They had to, she thought. There was no other way.

She finally fell asleep and slept until ten the next morning. She ate a piece of pizza for breakfast and stared at the pile of books she had to read parts of and her list of homework assignments. She wasn't up for that, though. She put on her swimsuit and hit the pool. The water felt good. The temperature was over one hundred degrees, so she spent most of her time in the pool.

When she realized she'd put off homework long enough, she dried off and hit the books. She worked late into the night again then finally climbed into bed, having finished every bit of her homework. That was good on one hand. On the other, it left her with nothing to do on Sunday but think of Crockett.

Gina got through the rest of the weekend, and Monday morning finally rolled around. She handed in her homework to Crockett as she filed into the classroom.

"I hope you enjoy it," she said.

"I'm sure I will."

Gina sat down and tried to focus on what Crockett was saying, but found herself fantasizing about her instead. She imagined making love in Crockett's office, on Crockett's desk. She could feel Crockett's strong hands covering her body. The fantasy ended at the sound of closing books and shuffling feet. She stood and made her way to the door.

"Ms. Moreno?" Crockett said. "May I see you in my office?"

The fantasy still fresh in her mind, Gina blushed.

"Sure," she said.

They walked down the hall in silence until they reached Crockett's office. Crockett stood aside and let Gina in.

"You didn't pay one bit of attention in class today," Crockett said.

Gina blushed again.

"What?" Crockett said.

Gina wasn't sure how honest to be. She decided to be brutally honest.

"I'm sorry," she said. "I was fantasizing about you."

"You were, were you?"

"Yes. I'm sorry. So, what was the assignment?"

"We reviewed chapter three in class, so you'll have to read it then answer the questions at the end."

"Okay. Sorry about that."

"No biggie. But you should remember you're still in that class until your advisor tells you you're not. So no more fantasizing. Focus."

"I understand."

"Okay. Now you'd better hurry or you'll be late to your next class."

CHAPTER SEVENTEEN

Tuesday morning, Gina was up with the dawn. She wasn't taking any chances on being late. She was up, dressed, and ready to go at seven o'clock. With nothing to do but chill, she sat at the table drinking coffee and thinking up ways to approach the subject. How would she explain her desire to drop the class? She'd think of something. She really didn't need a reason, she figured. She'd just ask and he'd let her switch to another class and it would be good.

At seven thirty, she picked up her backpack and started the walk to the student service center where she'd meet with Mr. Mouton. She found him in his office waiting for her. He stood when she came in and offered his hand.

"Hello, Ms. Moreno," he said.

"Hello."

"How can I help you?"

"I need to get out of one of my classes, so I'd like to transfer into another class."

"Which class did you need to get out of? And why?"

"Creative Fiction," Gina said. And why? She had to think and think quick. "I just don't think I'm ready for that class yet."

"Not ready? You're met all the prerequisites. You shouldn't have a problem."

"Still, I'd like to transfer out of it. Is there a class I can transfer into?"

"Let me check."

He clicked on his keyboard and stared at his monitor for what seemed like ages.

"Any class you could transfer into is full," he said. "We have a lot of grad students in the English department this semester."

"Well, then, I'd just like to drop the class, please."

There was more clicking at his keyboard.

"If you drop this class, Ms. Moreno, you won't have enough credits to qualify for your scholarship."

Gina felt as if someone had reached in her chest and pummeled her heart. This couldn't be happening. She couldn't afford to give up her scholarship.

"Do you have concerns about Professor Devine?" Mr. Mouton asked. "Because I can assure you she's very good."

Gina felt heat flow to her face and hoped he didn't notice. No one had to tell her how good Crockett was.

"No, sir," she said. "I don't have any problem with her."

"Good. I'm sorry I can't help you."

"Me too. Thank you for trying."

She got up and headed to her first class of the day. She met Melinda in her office.

"What's wrong?" Melinda said. "You look like you lost your best friend."

"I think I did."

"What? Why?"

"I just tried to transfer out of Creative Fiction and I can't."

"Oh, Gina. I'm so sorry."

"Yeah. I don't know what to do now."

"I'm sure you and Crockett will figure something out."

"I hope so."

They walked to class together and Gina took her place in the front of the class while Melinda taught. Gina let her mind wander during class. She tried to formulate another plan, but came up with nothing. She left that class and went to the rest of her classes, doing her best to focus in each one.

She left campus and was home studying when there was a knock on her door. She answered it to find Crockett standing there.

"Come in," she said.

"Well," Crockett said as soon as she was inside. "How'd it go?"

Gina couldn't help it. She fought to keep the burning in her eyes to just that, but it didn't work. She felt the tears flow and couldn't stop them.

"That good, huh?" Crockett took her in her arms. "Sh. Don't cry."

"Why not? There's nothing more we can do." Gina disengaged herself from Crockett. "And you holding me isn't helping."

"I'm sorry. I was just trying to comfort you."

"I know, but I can't handle your arms around me. Not now anyway."

"I get that. So, what do we do now?"

"I don't think there's anything we can do."

"You're giving up?" Crockett said.

"I don't know, Crockett. You have to teach the class and I have to take it, so where does that leave us?"

"Maybe I'll come down with some rare disease and miss the rest of the semester."

"Don't even joke like that."

"Well, then what?" Crockett said.

"I think we just have to accept that we can't see each other for a few months."

"Can't see each other except in the classroom three times a week?"

"You know what I mean. We can't keep being an item."

"But I like being an item with you," Crockett said.

"I like it, too. But we can't continue. You could get in all kinds of trouble."

"I know."

"So, we go on a break from each other."

"A break? What does that mean? We date other people? What?"

"I can't imagine dating anyone else," Gina said.

"Neither can I. I never thought I'd settle down and then you came along. But you're new in town. You're young. I can't ask you to sit at home and wait for the semester to be up."

"I'll be too busy with my schoolwork to be dating anyway."

"And if that's how it turns out, then fine. But I don't want you to pass up an opportunity, do you hear me?"

Gina's heart felt like it was breaking.

"You actually sound like you *want* me to date."

"No. Believe me, I'd rather you didn't, but I can't ask that of you. It wouldn't be fair."

"So, you're dumping me."

The tears began to flow again.

"It's not like that and you know it. We can't see each other, Gina. It's impossible. So I'm saying hopefully we get back together when the semester is over. But I can't ask you to wait until then for me. If someone comes along, I can't be responsible for you not pursuing it."

"No one's going to come along. And what about you? I guess this means you'll go back to your womanizing ways?"

"No. I can make it through the semester."

"But if you can't, it's okay, right, because we're split up?"

"I think you're missing the point," Crockett said.

"No. The point is we're split up. The same rules apply to you as apply to me. And it kills me to think of you with another woman."

"It kills me, too."

"Then don't say it's okay," Gina said.

"It has to be, Gina. We can't be seeing each other. We can't have commitments toward each other. This is the only solution."

Crockett stood, intent on leaving.

"I don't have to like it," Gina said.

"Neither do I. Now, I'll see you tomorrow in class. By the way, that was a nice story you wrote."

"I'm glad you liked it."

"I did. Very much. I've got to go. I'll see you tomorrow."

She left the apartment feeling like she'd left an appendage behind. She picked up her phone and called Melinda.

"Hey," Melinda said.

"What are you doing?"

"Nothing. Just getting ready for dinner. Why?"

"I just kind of don't want to be alone right now. You mind if I come over?"

"No problem. And we ordered Chinese for dinner, so there's plenty for you."

"Thanks, but I'm not really hungry."

"You okay?" Melinda said.

"Not really. I'll see you in a few."

She arrived at Melinda's house and let herself in, as was customary. She found Melinda and Terry in the family room watching television.

"You guys could have started on dinner," she said.

"No. We wanted to wait for you. But come on now. We're starving."

"Oh, then, by all means, let's go to the table. I don't suppose you have any beer here?" She'd noticed both of them sipping wine.

"Sure," Melinda said. "They're in the fridge. Help yourself."

Crockett grabbed one then joined them at the table. The food did smell good. She decided to have some. She was serving up when Melinda finally said something.

"So what's going on?"

"I just broke up with Gina," Crockett said.

"Well, you both knew it was coming, right?"

"We both worried it might be. But still, it felt so final."

"It's not really final, is it?" Terry said. "It's only until the semester is over."

"A semester lasts a long time."

"But still," Melinda said. "You two will get back together after the semester ends and it'll be just like before."

"We talked about that."

"And?" Melinda said.

"And I told her I don't want her to wait around for me. If she meets someone else, I want her to feel free to pursue it."

"Crockett," Melinda said. "How could you say something like that?"

"It's only fair." Crockett took a pull off her drink. "I can't ask her to be committed to me if we can't be together."

"That actually makes sense," Terry said.

"It does not," Melinda said. "It makes no sense. So you can see other people too, I'm guessing?"

"Theoretically .Of course, I have no desire to do that. She's young, though. And she's new to town. She's going to be meeting people. It's only fair that I let her be free."

"I for one, can only imagine how hurt she must be feeling right now."

"We both are. Which is why I didn't want to be alone. Although I have to admit, things ending this way were easier than they could have been. Who knows how things would have gone if we'd stayed together? We could have had a brutal breakup. So, for this, I'm thankful."

"You're always welcome here. And I doubt you'd have had a bad breakup. You two were great together."

Crockett took a bite of the kung pao chicken. It was good. She was surprised. She'd expected everything to taste like cardboard. She helped herself to an egg roll, amazed at how hungry she suddenly was.

"You know," Terry said. "We're having a little get-together this weekend with some friends of mine. You're more than welcome to join us."

"I've been meaning to ask you," Melinda said. "I just haven't seen much of you lately."

"Yeah," Crockett said. "The first couple of weeks of a semester are always the busiest. But I'd love to come to your shindig."

"Great. We're asking people to show up around five and we'll fire up the grill around six," Terry said.

"I can do that. What should I bring?"

"Why don't you bring some beer?" Melinda said.

"Sure. I'll bring a case of my favorite."

"That would be wonderful," Terry said.

Crockett left their house with a full stomach and a much better attitude. She got home late and had papers to grade. She got them done and crawled into bed at midnight. She was exhausted and fell into the hardest sleep she'd had in the last couple of weeks.

She woke the next morning full of dread. It would be the first time she'd seen Gina since the official breakup. She only hoped things would go smoothly. She showered, dressed, drank her coffee, and headed to school. She stopped by her office and checked her email. Nothing she had to deal with right then.

With apprehension creeping its way into her system again, she made her way down the hall to Creative Fiction. There was Gina in the back row, looking amazing. She was so beautiful. She took Crockett's breath away. But Crockett had a job to do, and Gina was no longer hers to ogle. She started class.

When class was over, she went to her office. She had just sat down at her desk when in walked Gina.

"Gina, really," Crockett said. "It's not a good idea for you to keep coming to my office."

"What if I have a question about the assignment?"

"Oh. I'm sorry. What's your question?"

"I don't have one," Gina said.

"We need to stay away from each other. It'll be hard in the beginning, I know. But it's the only thing that will make this feel better in the long run."

"I can't imagine it ever feeling better."

"I know. Me neither. But we have to be strong Gina. I can't afford to get in trouble."

"I don't want you to get in trouble," Gina said.

"Then please. For me. Honor our breakup."

"I will."

"Thank you."

Crockett watched Gina walk out of her office and felt her chest ache. She felt like her heart had just split in two.

The rest of the week went on with no real issues. Crockett had read and reread Gina's short story until she had it memorized. And as much as she liked it, she had to give it a B+. She didn't feel it was A material. But Gina definitely showed promise, which made Crockett feel good.

The weekend finally rolled around. Crockett was looking forward to hanging out with Terry and Melinda and some new people. It would give her a chance to get her mind off Gina. At least for a few hours.

As promised, she stopped by the store and picked up a case of her favorite beer. She arrived at Melinda's house shortly after five. It was already hard to find parking. She parked behind Terry's car in the driveway and got out.

She carried the beer around to the back of the house.

"Crockett," Melinda said. "You made it."

"I said I would. Where do you want this?" She held up the case of beer.

"There's an ice chest out here. Most of it should fit in it. Follow me."

As Crockett followed Melinda, she checked out the variety of people they had invited. Most were Terry's friends. They were all gay or lesbian, or so it seemed. There was some nice eye candy there. She couldn't or wouldn't touch, but she could certainly enjoy the view.

She filled the ice chest with beer. As she was bent over, she felt a hand on her ass. She stood so quickly, she almost dropped the beer in her hand. She turned to see Gabby standing there.

"Hey, Gabby," she said.

"Hey, Crockett. You know, you've got the finest ass I think I've ever seen."

"Thank you. That's always nice to hear."

"So where have you been? I haven't seen you in a while."

"I was seeing someone."

"As in past tense?" Gabby said.

"Yes. Past tense."

"I'm sorry, I guess. But that means you're available again and I do like the sound of that."

"I don't know that I'm ready to be available."

"Maybe you'll change your mind by the end of the night."

"I don't know…"

"Well," Gabby said. "I don't need an answer right now. For now, you should mingle. Go see and be seen, because believe me, you deserve to be seen."

Crockett watched Gabby walk off. She had to smile. It felt good to have someone attracted to her, but she wasn't looking for anything. She hadn't begun to get over Gina yet. And doubted she would.

She wandered through the crowd. There were about twenty people there. Everyone was laughing and enjoying themselves. She tried to relax, but was having a hard time. She took a drink off her beer and wandered over to where Terry was talking to two very attractive women.

"Oh, Crockett," Terry said. "Let me introduce you to my friends. This is Sasha and this is Monica."

"Nice to meet you." Crockett shook their hands. Sasha was full-figured with shoulder length brown hair and brown eyes. Monica was a strawberry blonde who had blue eyes. They were both very cute.

"Nice to meet you, too," they both said. Sasha's gaze moved over Crockett as she said it.

Crockett almost blushed at the brazenness. But Sasha was cute and Crockett needed someone to talk to. And there were no rules about talking to cute girls.

Terry walked off, leaving Crockett alone with them.

"So, how do you know Terry?" Crockett said.

"We used to babysit her kids," Sasha said. "How about you?"

"Melinda's been my best friend for years."

"Oh, that's great. She seems really good for Terry," Monica said. "By the way, where'd you get that beer?"

"I brought it. There's plenty in the ice chest by the grill. Help yourself."

"Thanks. You want one, Sasha?"

"Please."

"Okay. I'll be right back."

She walked off, leaving Crockett alone with Sasha.

"So, you and Monica," she said. "How long have you two been an item?"

Sasha laughed.

"Oh no. We're not together. Just best friends since we were kids."

"Oh. So you two aren't lesbians?"

"We are. Just not with each other. Wait. You know what I mean."

Crockett laughed.

"Yes. I do."

She liked Sasha. She was easy to talk to. And she was definitely easy on the eyes. She almost resented it when Monica was back with their beers.

"I should leave you two and go mingle," Crockett said.

"Why?" Sasha said. "Don't you like us?"

"Well, sure."

Crockett didn't miss the look Monica gave Sasha.

"Then hang out with us," Sasha said.

"Fine. If you're sure you don't mind."

"No. It'll be great," Monica said.

Crockett spent the rest of the evening with them, including sitting with them at dinner. She found her insides stirring at the thought of what could possibly happen with Sasha. She was disappointed when Monica announced it was time for them to leave. Sasha looked at Crockett questioningly, and Crockett knew it was time for her to make her move. All she had to do was say the word and Sasha would be hers.

"Well, it was nice meeting you," she said. "You two have a good night."

"Good night," they said in unison.

Crockett decided she should find Terry and Melinda and say good night to them. She needed to use the restroom first so turned down the hallway. Suddenly, she felt a hand on her arm and she turned to see Gabby there.

Gabby pressed herself against Crockett and kissed her hard on her mouth. Crockett felt herself responding at first. Then she gently pushed Gabby away.

"I'm sorry, Gabby. I can't...I just can't."

She didn't bother saying good night to her hostesses. She just got in her truck and drove home.

CHAPTER EIGHTEEN

It was Saturday afternoon several weeks after Crockett had unceremoniously dumped her, and Gina was deep in her studies when her phone rang.

"Hello?" she said.

"Hey, Gina. It's me, Donna."

"Oh, hi. I haven't heard from you in a while."

"I've been working out of town. But I was thinking about you and wondered how you were doing."

"I'm okay."

"Yeah? Just okay? Everything still going great with Crockett?"

Gina was silent. She didn't want to talk about it.

"Gina?"

"I'm here. Crockett and I split up."

"Oh man. That's too bad. I'm sorry to hear that."

"Thanks."

"So, what are you doin' now?" Donna said.

"Nothing. Homework."

"That's exciting."

"Isn't it?"

"Well, get showered and dressed. I'll be over in an hour. We'll do dinner and hit the club."

"I don't think so, Donna. I'm not really up for that."

"Aw, come on. When was the last time you went out?"

"I don't know," Gina said.

"It'll be good for you. We'll have fun."

"Really—"

"I'm not taking no. I'll be there in an hour."

The line went dead.

Shit, Gina thought. She wasn't ready to go out. But then again, Donna might have a point. Getting out might not be such a bad idea. She bookmarked where she was in her textbook, closed her laptop, and headed to the shower.

She took her time and was ready just before Donna arrived. She had just poured a glass of wine when she heard the knock on her door. She opened the door to find Donna in her usual carpenter shorts and oxford shirt. She looked good, but Gina knew she did, too.

"Come on in. I just poured myself a glass of wine. Would you like something to drink?"

"I'd love a beer if you have one."

"I do. Have a seat. I'll get it for you."

She went to the refrigerator and took out a beer. It didn't feel right to be giving one of Crockett's beers to Donna, but she wasn't going to drink them so why not? She walked out to the living room to see Donna on the couch next to where Gina had been sitting. Gina didn't want to sit that close to her. She handed Donna her beer and picked up her glass of wine and moved to the loveseat.

"I don't bite," Donna said.

"I'm just more comfortable over here."

"Suit yourself."

They chatted as they drank their beverages. Donna had been working in the Bay Area for several weeks. She told Gina all about where she'd been and what she'd seen.

"I went to San Francisco for a day with Crockett," Gina said.

"Oh. Then, never mind. I guess we'll talk about something else."

"No. I don't mind. It's interesting hearing it from you."

They finished their drinks and headed out to Donna's truck. Donna took her to Tres Hombres, the same Mexican restaurant

Gina had gone to with Crockett. She fought hard to get her food down as memories of better times flooded over her.

"What's the matter?" Donna said. "Aren't you hungry?"

"I guess I'm not as hungry as I thought I was. I'm working on it, though."

"You can always take some home."

"Yeah, that's true."

She did her best and managed to eat most of her meal with the help of her two margaritas. She was feeling better when they left to go to the club. She wasn't sure how she'd feel about dancing with someone besides Crockett, but Crockett had kicked her to the curb and she had to remember that. She was free to do as she pleased. But it still felt odd.

The place was fairly empty when they got there, so they were able to get a table by the floor. Donna went up and ordered them more margaritas while Gina kept her focus on the crowd. She realized she was holding her breath, hoping to see Crockett walk in. But she didn't. Crockett didn't show up. It was just Donna and her and a bunch of strangers.

Donna and Gina talked while the music was still at a lower volume, but once it got turned up too high, Donna asked Gina to dance. Again, waves of guilt washed over Gina, but she forced them down and walked to the floor with Donna. Once she started moving it was easy to forget her worries and just move to the music. She danced and grooved through several songs, almost forgetting that Donna was on the floor with her. The music slowed and Donna opened her arms, but Gina shook her head and walked back to the table.

Donna got them more drinks while Gina went back to surveying the crowd. Donna actually startled her when she returned as Gina was lost in people watching.

"Are you having fun?" Donna said.

"Actually, I am."

"Great. I'm glad to hear that. See? I told you it would be good to get out."

"And you were right. Now let's go dance some more."

Donna took another quick sip of her drink and Gina led them to the floor. They danced for another few songs until Gina was thirsty. They went back to the table and finished their drinks.

"I'll get us a couple more," Donna said.

"No, thanks. I think I'd like to go home now."

"Are you sure? The night is still young."

"Yeah, but I'm tired."

"Okay. We can leave."

They drove back to Gina's apartment and Gina started to get out of the truck.

"Aren't you going to invite me in for a beer?" Donna said.

Gina thought about it. It would be polite.

"Sure," she said. "Come on in."

She wasn't really in the mood to socialize anymore, but it would be rude to not invite Donna in. Where was the harm in it?

They went inside and Donna sat on the couch while Gina got them their drinks. Gina walked out and handed Donna hers while she sat across from her on the loveseat. Donna picked up her beer and sat next to Gina.

"See?" she said. "Isn't this better?"

"Donna…"

"It's okay. I'm not doing anything."

"And I don't want you to. Look, I don't mean to seem ungrateful or anything. But I'm not ready for anything more than a night out."

She saw Donna's face fall. She recovered quickly, but Gina had already seen the disappointment in her eyes.

"I'm sorry, Donna."

"No. It's all good. I'm just glad you had fun tonight."

"I really did. And I appreciate you doing that for me."

"No problem. I'll check back with you later and take you out again if you're up for it."

"That would be nice," Gina said.

Donna set her beer down.

"I'd probably better get going."

"Okay,"

Gina walked her to the door. Donna leaned in and kissed her on the cheek.

"Take care, Gina."

"You too."

"I will."

Gina watched her walk out to her truck then closed the door. She'd had such a good time. Why had it had to end like that? And why had she felt guilty having Donna in her apartment so late at night? Because she knew what Donna wanted. And somewhere deep inside, Gina had wanted it too. But it would have felt like she was cheating on Crockett. Crockett. The woman who had dumped her. How could she have cheated on her? She shook her head and got ready for bed, but sleep didn't come. Instead she played over times that she hadn't had to spend the night alone.

She ran her hands over her body, remembering how Crockett had touched her just so. She shivered as memories overcame reality and she lost herself in the fantasies. Her breathing became labored as she touched herself, bringing herself to an orgasm that felt amazing yet empty. She missed Crockett.

❖

Football season was in full swing. Chico State didn't have a football team, but that was okay with Crockett. She was a diehard Oregon Duck fan. Her cousin had gone to Oregon when she was a kid and she'd stayed true to them her whole life. She was watching the game at home one Saturday afternoon when she grew tired and bored. She turned off the television at halftime and drove to The Oasis to watch the second half. She ordered a cheeseburger and fries and a half pitcher of Great White beer. The food was good and the beer was cold. She sat at the bar watching the game when she felt a hand on her back. She turned to see Sasha standing there.

"I thought that was you, Crockett."

"Well, hey there, Sasha. How have you been?"

"I've been great. How about you?"

"Not bad."

"Good. Do you want to come join us at our table?"

"I'll tell you what. The game's almost over. When it ends I'll join you, okay?"

"That sounds good. We plan on being here for a while."

Crockett finished watching the game, then ordered a pitcher of beer and wandered over to Sasha and Monica's table.

"I hope you like Great White," she said as she put the pitcher down.

"I'll drink it, but Monica will only drink wine."

"Fair enough. More for us. Where is Monica anyway?"

"She's over there playing pool."

"Ah. Is she any good?"

"We can both hold our own," Sasha said.

"Why don't you play doubles?"

"I got bored. Maybe later."

"I should put some quarters up."

"You play pool?"

"I can hold my own." Crockett smiled.

"Somehow I was really surprised to see you here. We come here all the time. I wonder why I've never seen you here before."

"Maybe you did before we met and you just never noticed."

"Oh, I'd have noticed," Sasha said.

"Is that right?" Crockett grinned. Was she flirting? Like actually flirting? She was. She felt a momentary pang of guilt, but quickly quelled it. She wasn't doing anything wrong. She was just enjoying the company of a beautiful woman. Who wasn't Gina. But Gina was no longer hers. She told herself to relax and have some fun.

"I'm going to go get some quarters to put on the table," she said. She walked up to the bar and could feel Sasha's gaze on her. She smiled to herself as she handed the bartender a ten and asked for a roll of quarters.

She turned to catch Sasha in the act, but Sasha quickly turned away and pretended to be engrossed in the pool game. Crockett swallowed a laugh. She put her quarters on the table.

"Oh, hi, Crockett," Monica said.

"Hi, Monica. How are you doing?"

"Good. I'm about to win again, so you may be playing against me."

"Sounds like a plan."

Crockett walked back to the table and poured herself a glass of beer. It felt good going down. She poured a glass for Sasha, too.

"Thanks," Sasha said.

"I hope you'll like it."

"Oh, I know I will. It's one of my favorite beers."

"Good."

The pool game ended and Crockett racked the balls for Monica. Sasha came over by the pool table to watch.

"Just out of curiosity," Monica said. "Who are you rooting for, Sasha?"

"I just want to watch a good game."

"I call bullshit."

Crockett laughed out loud.

"Come on," she said. "Let's play."

Crockett ended up wiping the table with Monica.

"No fair," Monica said. "I didn't know you were a shark."

"So I got lucky."

"You two want to play doubles?" a man asked.

"Sure," Crockett said. "I mean, it's fine by me. What about you, Monica?"

"Sounds good to me."

Crockett poured herself some more beer while the man racked the balls.

"You want to go first?" she asked Monica.

"Heck no. I want you to go and finish them the first break."

Crockett laughed. She was really enjoying herself.

"I don't know if I can do that, but I'll give it my best shot."

Crockett broke and, sure enough, ran the table. The guys walked off and there were no more challengers.

"So what about you, Sasha?" Crockett said. "Do you want to play me?"

"Yeah. Come on, Sash," Monica said. "Why not?"

"Sure, why not indeed? I don't mind public humiliation."

She racked the balls.

"Maybe I'll go easy on you," Crockett said.

"Maybe you two should get a room," Monica said.

Crockett grinned at her, but told herself that maybe she was flirting too hard-core. She didn't really expect anything to happen with Sasha. But then again, she was a free woman and if something happened then it did. She didn't have to answer to anyone.

She broke and followed up with several shots, almost clearing the table of solids.

"Gee," Monica said. "Thanks for going easy on me."

"Sorry."

Monica knocked in quite a few of the striped balls and left Crockett in a bad position. But Crockett did a trick shot and knocked in the last of her balls. She sunk the eight ball and proclaimed victory.

Sasha slapped her playfully on the arm.

"No fair. You're better than you said you are."

"I said I could hold my own. And I can. Let's get another pitcher and chill for a while." She turned to Monica. "You want another wine?"

"Yes, please."

She went to the bar, ordered the drinks, then came back to the table. Monica sat on one bench and Crockett and Sasha sat on the other. Sasha sat closer to Crockett than was necessary, but they weren't touching. Still, Crockett was very aware of her. She could feel the heat radiating off her. She told herself to be cool. Everything was okay.

"So, how did you hear of this place?" Monica asked. "Did you hear about it from your students?"

"Heck no. I used to come here all the time when I was a student. They have the best burgers in town. And the price is right. I don't get here as often as I should, but I try to get here once in a while."

"Well, I'm glad you came today," Sasha said.

"Me, too."

Monica went up to the bar and got some dice cups so they could play games. Crockett was holding her own there, too, but she did have to drink several times. She was feeling no pain and knew she'd probably better get out of there while she could still drive. She was relieved when Monica suggested they call it a night.

"You could always come over to our place for a post party," Sasha said.

"And if I partied anymore, how would I drive home?"

"Who said you'd have to leave our place?" Sasha grinned and moved closer to Crockett. Crockett could smell her perfume and feel her warmth again. She stood still contemplating what Sasha had said.

Sasha ran her hands up Crockett's check and around her neck. She pulled her head down. Just before their lips met, Crockett was overcome with guilt. She removed Sasha's hands from her.

"I'm sorry, Sasha. Don't get me wrong. I think you're hot and I'm really into you. I'm just not ready yet. Maybe next time, okay?"

Sasha looked crestfallen, then embarrassed.

"Wow," Monica said. "Talk about a tease."

"Look. I didn't mean to lead you on."

"I call bullshit," Monica said. That seemed to be her favorite phrase.

"Okay, so maybe I did. And maybe I thought I could follow through. But I can't. At least not tonight. I really am sorry."

She turned and got in her truck and drove home.

CHAPTER NINETEEN

Crockett stood in front of her class of Creative Fiction on Friday morning.

"I know we're all excited to have next week off and I hope everyone has a safe and fun Thanksgiving. But remember, I gave you an assignment at the beginning of this week that's due when you get back. I need a ten-thousand-word story. It's due the thirtieth. You can email it to me anytime. I'll be checking my emails throughout the week. Or you can simply hand it in next Monday."

She dismissed her class and went to her office for office hours. She heard a knock on her door and looked up from the computer to see Melinda standing there.

"Hey, Melinda. What's up?"

"I'm just making sure you're still coming over for Thanksgiving dinner Thursday."

"I wouldn't miss it."

"Good. Oh, and fair warning, Sasha will be there."

"She will, will she?" Crockett grinned. She thought of Sasha and how much fun they'd had together at The Oasis that day.

"Yeah. I understand something happened between you two and I don't want it to be awkward for you."

"No, Melinda. Nothing happened between us, although I may have led her to believe something would. So, yeah, it might be awkward at first, but I'm sure we'll both get over it."

"Oh. Well, I didn't know the whole story."

"Don't worry about it."

"Okay. So I'll see you Thursday."

"What do you want me to bring?" Crockett said.

"Beer, please."

"Will do. What time should I be there?"

"We're suggesting two o'clock. We can watch football and socialize until dinner at four."

"Most excellent. I'll see you there."

Crockett sat back in her chair after Melinda had walked off. Sasha would be there, huh? It had been so long since she'd been with a woman, she just might give in to Sasha's charms. And why not? Sasha was adorable and obviously attracted to her, too. They were both adults. Suddenly, Thursday was looking better.

She finished her day and was relieved at the week off ahead of her. Nine whole days without students. It would be so nice. She went home, took a nap, then took herself out for dinner and headed to the club. She was in the mood to dance and celebrate.

There were quite a few people there when she got there. She took a seat at the bar and checked out the crowd. There were quite a few familiar faces. One in particular caught her attention. She crossed through the crowd to her.

"Hey, Gabby," Crockett said.

Gabby turned around and her face broke into a wide smile.

"Well, hello, Crockett. Fancy seeing you here."

"I'm celebrating Thanksgiving break."

"Good for you. You want to dance?"

"Sure."

They made their way through the throng on the dance floor and found a place to move to the music. Crockett enjoyed watching Gabby dance, though she didn't focus only on her. The music sounded so good and it felt so good to be dancing that she lost herself in it all. They'd danced several dances before a slow song came on. Gabby arched an eyebrow at Crockett who smiled.

"Not yet, my dear," Crockett said. She walked Gabby back to her table. "Can I buy you a drink?"

"Sure."

Crockett came back with drinks.

"Do you mind if I join you?" she asked.

"That depends."

"On what?"

"On if you're going to lead me on or if there's a payoff in it for me."

Crockett thought long and hard. She took a deep pull off her beer. Did she really want to sleep with Gabby? Or did she just want some fun and flirting? Again, it had been so long since she'd shared her bed with a woman. On the other hand, the semester was almost over. But the semester being over was no guarantee Gina would still be available. Damn. She was pretty much fucked either way. Or not.

"Then I guess I'd better move on," Crockett said. "It was good seeing you again."

She left her beer on the table and exited the bar.

Crockett graded papers from all her classes the rest of the weekend and into the new week. She kept checking for a paper from Gina but there wasn't one in her inbox.

Thursday rolled around, and Crockett took her time getting ready. She was really excited to see Sasha. She only hoped Sasha wouldn't be too mad at her. She was so cute and so much fun. She just hoped they could flirt without expectation. Although she was tempting, oh so tempting. When she had her arms around Crockett at The Oasis, Crockett had almost kissed her. But she knew if she had, there would be no turning back. And Crockett hadn't been ready at that point to seal the deal. Today? Who knew?

She showered and dressed in slacks and a long-sleeved button down shirt. She felt good and was ready to hit the road. She grabbed the beer she'd bought the day before and drove to Melinda's house.

As usual, Crockett let herself in. She walked to the kitchen to find Melinda preparing several dishes at once.

"Do you need any help?" she asked.

"No, thanks. I'm fine. Just put the beer in the ice chest and find a place to get comfortable."

Crockett did as instructed. She took a beer and headed toward the sound of the voices coming from the great room. Her gaze immediately landed on Sasha. There was an empty seat next to her. The television was across from her with the game on. She cut across the room.

Sasha looked up at her. Her cheeks turned a slight shade of pink.

"Hi, Crockett."

"Hey, Sasha. Can I sit here?"

"Please do."

The people around them cheered at a touchdown.

"Are we okay?" Crockett said quietly.

"I don't know. I guess that's up to you. I'm the one who made a fool of myself."

"No, you didn't. You made me an offer I couldn't accept, unfortunately. But I really want us to be okay now."

"Okay. Then we are."

"Good." Crockett patted her leg. It was warm to her touch. She felt herself become hot. She needed to calm down. It was going to be a long afternoon.

She settled in to watch the game, ever aware of Sasha sitting next to her. When she needed another beer, she offered one to Sasha.

"Please," Sasha said.

Crockett went to the ice chest to get a beer.

"Are you fucking with her again?" Monica said.

"What? No."

"I call bullshit." There was that phrase again. "She felt like a fool the last time we saw you, and I blame you more than her."

"I do too."

"You do?"

"Sure. I admit I led her on. I was having so much fun with her. But when push came to shove, I couldn't do it. It was all me, not her. Believe me."

"Have you told her that yet?"

"Not in so many words, but yes."

"Good. Because she's my best friend and I'll do anything to protect her."

"You don't need to protect her from me. I promise."

"I'd better not."

Crockett grabbed the two beers and headed back to the great room. She handed one to Sasha and took a drink off the other one. They relaxed and watched football until Melinda called them to dinner.

Melinda had outdone herself, as usual. The turkey was delicious and Crockett had some of every side dish. When she was through, she thought she might explode.

"That was amazing," she said.

The table joined together, voicing their agreement.

"It really was amazing, sweetheart," Terry said. She stood and began clearing the table. Crockett got up and helped. Soon, Sasha was in the kitchen with them and the three of them set about getting things cleaned up.

Every time Sasha brushed against Crockett in the kitchen, Crockett felt heat wash over her. It was like an electrical shock went through her. Sasha was dangerous to her. She thought about taking her home and having her way with her. But then, Sasha didn't really seem like the one-night stand kind of woman. And Crockett wouldn't be looking for anything more. She didn't even know if she was looking for a one-night stand.

After the cleanup was complete, people started making their way out. Monica walked up to Crockett.

"I won't let her ask you over again, so if you want anything from her, you're the one who's going to have to do the asking."

MJ W<small>ILLIAMZ</small>

"I understand," Crockett said. "Look, you need to understand that I like Sasha. I like her a lot. Which is just one of the reasons I can't be with her."

"Whatever."

Crockett just stared at Monica and realized she should be having the conversation with Sasha. She found her in the great room and gently took her by the arm and led her down the hall for some privacy.

"Look, Sasha," she said. "I really like you."

"That's fair. Because, obviously, I like you, too."

"I'm just not in a position to offer myself up for a relationship. It's complicated."

"It always is."

"I know. It sounds cliché, but I can't do it. And it wouldn't be fair to either of us for me to take you home for one night. You're not that kind of person and I can't be more than that."

"Well, at least you're being honest with me," Sasha said.

"I'm trying. I like you. And I wish I was free to pursue something with you. I really do. But I'm not."

"Okay. Whatever's going on with you is your business. But if you ever decide you're seriously interested in me, let me give you my number."

Crockett handed her phone to Sasha who entered her phone number.

"Thanks," Crockett said.

"Take care, Crockett."

"You, too."

Crockett watched as Sasha and Monica said their good-byes and left. She tried to convince herself she'd done the right thing, but she wasn't looking forward to another lonely night in her empty bed.

❖

Gina was relieved to have a week off of school. It meant a week of not seeing Crockett, which would do her a world of good.

It still drove her crazy to see Crockett at the front of the classroom three days a week, looking all dapper and knowing she couldn't have her. She often wondered if Crockett was seeing anybody, but she doubted it. But then she'd wonder if Crockett had gone to the club and hooked up with another woman. That was more likely, and the thought of it made Gina's skin crawl. But Crockett had made it plain that they could see other people, so she probably had had several women over the semester. Gina hoped not, but knew Crockett. She'd been a womanizer before they'd gotten together. What was to keep her from being one since they'd split?

She packed her things and got ready to spending the week with her parents. They'd begged her to come home for the holiday. She really didn't want to go. And she'd explained to them she'd probably spend most of her time on her laptop doing school work. But they'd still insisted, so she packed her winter clothes and prepared for a horrible week.

Gina wondered how Crockett was spending the holiday. They should be spending it together. She hoped Crockett wouldn't be alone. But she reasoned she was probably going to Melinda's for the day. They were so close and Melinda would never let Crockett be alone.

Her flight to Chicago was uneventful. Her father picked her up. There was no hug or anything. He put her bags in the back of the SUV and they got in.

"How was your flight?" he asked.

"It was nice. How are you and Mom?"

"We're fine. Your sister and her family will be over for Thanksgiving Day."

"Oh, good. It'll be good to see them."

"So, you have a lot of homework?" he said.

"I do. We're coming close to the end of the semester so there are lots of papers and assignments due. I have to write a ten-thousand-word story for one of my classes."

"Sounds hard."

"We'll see."

"You really like it in California, huh?" he said.

"I do. Chico is a cute town and the campus is gorgeous. I'm enjoying my time there." The last bit didn't really apply at the moment, but the last thing she wanted to talk to her parents about was the affair she'd been having with an assistant professor.

The rest of the forty-five-minute drive was spent in silence. Gina's stomach was in knots. Why had she agreed to come back here for the holiday? She wouldn't be comfortable. And she had a new life in a new location where she was comfortable. Lonely, sure, but comfortable. She would have been happy to spend the week in her apartment working on her assignments. The thought of working on Crockett's assignment in her parents' home scared her. What if someone saw it? She'd planned on writing a short romance between two women. And she didn't want her parents or her nosy sister seeing it. Oh, well. She was there now and figured she'd just have to make the best of it.

They arrived at the ranch style house and Gina's dad got her bags out and carried them in for her.

"Maria," he called. "We're home."

Gina's mom came out of the kitchen to greet them.

"Oh, Gina," she said. "It's so good to see you. It looks like California has been good to you."

"So far, so good."

"I'm so glad to hear that. Tony, put her things in her room."

Her room. It was her old room. Her room was in her apartment. And it was a lonely space. She was sure her room here would feel equally as lonely if not more so. She was missing Crockett more than she'd anticipated. Sure, she couldn't have her, but at least in Chico she got to see her three times a week, torture though it was. She thought it would be a relief to get away from her for a week, but clearly, she'd been wrong.

"Come on in," her mom said. "Don't stand in the entryway. Dinner's almost ready. Pour yourself a glass of wine and visit with me while I finish the salad."

She poured herself a glass of red wine.

"Dinner smells good," Gina said.

"It's your favorite. Grandma's lasagna."

Gina almost choked on her wine. The first meal she'd ever made for Crockett. She wished she could get her out of her head.

"Sounds great," Gina said.

"So, tell me. Have you met any nice young men out there?"

Gina cringed. Why couldn't they accept she was a lesbian? She thought about pointing that out to her mom, but then figured why cause a battle?

"Not yet. But I've been pretty busy with school."

"You know what they say about all work and no play."

"I'll have time to play after I get my master's."

"You're not getting any younger."

"No. I don't suppose I am."

Her dad was back and he mixed himself and her mom martinis.

"What have I missed?" he asked.

"Nothing. Your daughter hasn't found a suitor yet."

"Give her time."

"Thanks, Dad."

"Not too much time," he said. "But time to get settled in at least."

They had dinner with no more personal questions and after, Gina excused herself to go do homework. She decided first off to work on her easy assignments. She got them done and started her story for Crockett. It was a story of star-crossed lovers. She thought it appropriate. It was about two women who loved each other deeply but couldn't be together. She got it half written before she climbed into bed, exhausted.

The next few days, Gina played dutiful daughter and helped her mother get things ready for Thanksgiving. She helped make pies and prep side dishes. She spent her nights working on her story for Crockett. The time was passing almost pleasantly.

Thursday arrived and Gina's sister and family arrived at the house for the big dinner. Jo was four years Gina's senior. She was already married with two children. She was the good one. Gina had known that since she was a little girl. And sure enough, her parents made all over her when she got there. Her and the kids. And her husband. Suddenly, it was as if Gina wasn't there. One more day, she told herself. Only one more day and she'd be able to fly home. She just needed to get through the day.

Dinner was good and Gina, to get away from everyone, cleared the table and did the dishes. She'd just finished when her mom came in.

"Come say good-bye to Jo and her family," she said.

Gina did as she was told. She was happy to see them go. She hated to feel that way, but she couldn't help it. Once they were gone, she excused herself to do homework. She finished her story for Crockett and slipped into bed, grateful she'd be going home the next day. She told herself the first thing she'd do when she got home was email Crockett her story. She only hoped she liked it. If she'd moved on, she might not enjoy the story at all. But if there was any chance she still cared for Gina, hopefully she'd read in Gina's story that she still cared for her as well.

Chapter Twenty

Crockett had only received a few stories back from her Creative Fiction class and almost didn't bother to check her email Saturday. But when she opened it she was pleased to see Gina's assignment in her inbox. She was excited to read it, but also somewhat apprehensive. What if the story told her of Gina's desire to be with someone else? She told herself not to be ridiculous. It didn't matter what Gina's story's theme was. It was a work of fiction.

She opened the story and started reading. The thing that struck her first was how much Gina's writing had improved over the course of the semester. That was after she'd read the first couple of paragraphs. The next thing that struck her was the message in her story. It was the tale of two women in love who couldn't be together. Could that possibly be Gina and Crockett she was writing about? She dared to hope. But then again, had they been in love? If so, were they still? Or would they still be at the end of the semester?

Crockett told herself she was being ridiculous. It was just a story. But she couldn't shake the feeling that there was hope for them yet. She reread the story several times, and each time, her heart fluttered with hope anew. She heard several more pings and knew she had more stories to read and papers to check. Students were sending them in close to the deadline, but still before. That was nice. She read Gina's story once more before deciding on the email to send to her with her grade.

Normally, she would write a critique and point out the good and bad in the story and then offer encouragement and give the grade. What she wanted to tell Gina was that her message had come through loud and clear. That she had remained faithful and longed to be with her at the end of the semester. But she couldn't. In the end, she kept it short, sweet, and professional.

"Your writing has really improved over the course of the semester. This was a very well written piece. You get an A."

She reread her response several times before finally hitting the send button. There. It was gone. She had to move on to the rest of her email. She tried to focus, to give each story her undivided attention, but it wasn't easy. Her mind kept drifting back to Gina's story. She finally gave up, printed it out, and put it in her desk drawer so she could read it whenever she wanted.

She went on to grade some more stories and a few papers from her other classes. Most of them were of B quality. She considered herself a good assistant professor and took it personally if, with four weeks or so left in the semester, her students' writing was still subpar.

When she'd finished with everything in her inbox, she made dinner and settled in with Archie to watch some television. Her phone rang.

"Hey, Melinda. What's up?" she said.

"Hey. Terry and I are going to the Montrose. Do you want to go?"

"Isn't it a little early?"

"That's why I'm calling you now. So you can get all spiffed up and go with us."

"Sure. That sounds great."

"Good. We'll meet you there at nine?"

"I'll be there."

Crockett hung up and went to take a nice long shower. She dried off and put on a pair of Dockers with a long-sleeved shirt. She couldn't wait to see Melinda. She wanted to tell her about Gina's story and get her opinion about it.

She got there after Melinda and Terry. They were already at a table when she walked in.

"Look at you," Melinda said. "Lookin' good."

"Thanks. So are you two."

"We're in our club clothes," Terry laughed.

"Yeah. Me, too. I'm going to go to the bar to get a beer. I'll be right back."

She bought her beer and went back to the table.

"So, Melinda, I'm so glad you called. I have to tell you what happened today."

"Oh, is it juicy?" Melinda smiled.

"No. Yes. I don't know."

"Well, that's definite," Terry said.

"I was grading stories and papers today," Crockett said.

"Who wasn't?" Melinda said.

"Well, I read the story Gina sent in. Guess what it's about?"

"What?"

"Two women who fall in love and then can't be together."

"Two women who fell in love, huh? Were you two in love?" Melinda said.

"That's not really the point here, is it?"

"So what happened in the story?" Terry said.

"The two women overcame their obstacles and were able to live happily ever after."

"Sounds like a great story," Melinda said. "Let me guess. You want me to tell you it was about the two of you?"

"I don't know. I mean, it sure felt like it, you know? Like she was sending me a message."

"Maybe she was. But I certainly hope you graded her story on content and not on your fantasy."

"I did. She's a damned good writer."

"I'm sure."

"No. I mean she is."

"No, I believe you," Melinda said. "She's smart. She's been a great TA. I'm going to be bummed when the semester ends and I'll have to break in a new one."

"But you think maybe she was talking about us? I mean, seriously?"

"Crockett, I don't want to get your hopes up. And I didn't read the story, so how could I honestly say?"

"Wait. Do you know something? Has she said something to you?"

"No. We don't talk about you. That's an unspoken rule."

"Okay. Good." Crockett relaxed. Melinda hadn't been much help, but she'd still believe Gina was available and open to getting back together after the semester ended. If only she could get through the last few weeks.

Gina's stomach was in knots when she saw the email from Crockett in her inbox. She wondered what she would say. Would she admit she'd seen the similarity between them and the women in the story? Would she tell her to hang in there until the end of the semester? Or would she tell her she was seeing someone? She felt like she might throw up.

She poured herself a glass of wine, opened the email, and saw the brief message from Crockett. What the hell did it mean? It didn't give anything away. What was she supposed to read from it? That Crockett wasn't interested? She wanted to cry. Her phone rang.

"Hello, Donna."

"Hey, Gina. How are you?"

"I'm okay. How are you?"

"Just okay. What's up? How was your trip back home?"

"That was awful. Thanks for asking."

"Is something else bothering you?" Donna said.

"It's nothing. I'm being stupid."

"Tell me."

"I just got an email from Crockett."

"Oh, really? That's interesting."

"No," Gina said. "Not that kind of an email."

"What kind then?"

"It was in response to a story I sent in for class. She sent me a short email with my grade. It's what she always does."

"Okay. So what's the big deal?"

"Nothing. Never mind," Gina said. "Forget I brought it up."

"No. I want to be here for you, but clearly I'm missing something."

"The story was about two women who fell in love and then couldn't be together, but got together in the end."

"Ah. So what you're hoping with her then?"

"Exactly."

"And she didn't give a hint at your happily ever after prospects?"

"Exactly again."

"Well, Gina, she really couldn't. She has to keep herself distanced from you. Anything hinting at her feelings for you could get her in a lot of trouble. Especially if it's on an email sent from her school's email address."

"Yeah. That makes sense. Thanks, Donna."

"Happy to help. So you feel like going to the club tonight?"

"I don't know, Donna. The last time we went didn't end well."

"It did. I just tried not to respect your boundaries. And I'm sorry for that. Tonight I will know better. You clearly still care very much for Crockett. And I really hope things will work out for you two."

"Thanks. Maybe a night out wouldn't be so bad."

"Okay. I'll pick you up at nine and we'll head over to the club."

"Okay. I'll be ready."

Gina hung up feeling much better. Donna was a good sounding board. She only hoped Donna would be true to her word and not try to hit on her again.

She made herself a little dinner and showered and dressed. She wore black leggings, a cream colored tunic sweater, and black boots. She felt good as she poured herself another glass of wine and waited for Donna to arrive.

Donna got there at precisely nine o'clock. She looked good in chinos and a sweater. She let out a low wolf whistle when she saw Gina.

"Damn, you look good, woman. I know. I said I'd respect your boundaries and I will, but damn, I can at least appreciate how good you look, right?"

If Gina had been inclined to blush, she's sure she would have at that moment. Instead she simply smiled.

"Thank you," she said. She went into the kitchen to get Donna a beer. She came back out to find Donna seated on the loveseat, across from where Gina had left her wine. That was a good sign. Gina handed Donna her beer and sat down to drink her wine.

They finished their drinks and drove to the bar. They pulled into the parking lot and Gina tensed visibly.

"What's up?" Donna said.

"Crockett's here."

"What do you want to do? Do you want me to take you home?"

Gina considered her options. She could go home and spend a nice, quiet evening at home or she could go inside and be tortured by watching Crockett dance with other women. But what if Crockett danced with her? What if, since they were still on break, they could dance and enjoy each other's company? But what if she didn't? Would Gina be strong enough to handle it?

"Gina?" Donna said. "What do you want to do?"

"We're here," Gina said. "We may as well go in."

"Okay. Let's do it then."

They walked in and the place was somewhat crowded. Gina looked around and immediately spotted Crockett at a table with Melinda and Terry. Her back was to Gina, which made Gina feel better. Gina took a seat while Donna went to get them drinks. She never took her eyes off Crockett's table. Melinda looked over and made eye contact. She looked startled and quickly looked away. Gina was about to look away when Crockett turned and their gazes met. Gina's heart did a somersault. She needed Crockett so desperately. She only hoped tonight they could forget their stupid student-teacher relationship and just be two women who cared about each other.

Crockett approached their table. She got there just as Donna arrived with their drinks.

"Hello, Gina," she said. "And Donna."

Gina saw the way she looked at Donna and then back to her. She thought they were an item. She had to be able to convince her they weren't. But how without sounding like an idiot?

"How was your break?" Gina asked.

"It was nice. Lots of work to do, but it was still nice. How was yours? What did you do?"

"It was horrible. I went back home to Illinois." She shuddered. "It wasn't much fun, but I did my daughterly duty."

"Well, I won't continue to interrupt your time together," Crocket said.

"It's no interruption," Donna said. "Pull up a seat. I'll go buy you a beer."

Crockett sat and Gina could sense her discomfort.

"So, did you want to dance?" Gina said.

"I don't think that would be such a good idea."

"No? Why not? We're on a break from school. One dance won't hurt."

"What about Donna?" Crockett said.

"What about her?"

"Don't you think she might get upset if you're dancing with someone else?"

"Heck no. We're just friends, Crockett."

"That's what you think. Are you sure she knows that?"

"Positive."

"All the same," Crockett said. "I don't think we should dance. You know the rules."

"But—"

"No buts. Rules are rules."

Donna was back with her beer.

"Thanks," Crockett said. "I hate to be a heel, but I think I'd better go now."

"Stay and drink your beer, Crockett," Donna said.

Crockett looked at Gina and Gina's heart melted. Her eyes said everything her mouth wouldn't or couldn't. She still had feelings for her. Gina had no doubt. Crockett sat down and her leg brushed Gina's. Gina felt the currents flow through it. She'd missed Crockett's touch. Even an incidental leg brush was a touch and Gina craved more.

She fought not to run her hand up Crockett's leg, to lay it on her thigh. It was a struggle. Instead, she leaned her leg against Crockett's. Crockett shifted away. Damn, Gina thought. She really wasn't interested, was she? But the look she'd given her. The way her eyes looked into her soul told her otherwise. Gina was more confused by the minute.

"Why don't you two get out there and dance?" Donna said.

"That wouldn't be a good idea," Crockett said.

"Why not? You're two consenting adults, aren't you?"

"I'm still her professor," Crockett said. "And I can't be seen dancing with her. Now, it's been a pleasure talking to you two. Thanks for the beer."

Gina watched Crockett walk off and felt her crotch clench. She wanted her so bad it hurt.

She realized Donna was watching her.

"How much longer in the semester?" Donna asked.

"Something like three weeks."

"You can do it, Gina. You can make it that long."

"Yeah, but you saw her. She didn't want to dance with me. What if she's seeing someone else?"

"Who, Gina? Who is she here with? Friends."

"Still, you never know."

"I think you should relax. I think she'll be yours again soon."

"I wish I had your faith," Gina said. "But I'm scared. Very scared."

"It'll all be over in three weeks. Then you'll know if you're back together or if you're starting over. But at least you'll know."

"I don't want to start over," Gina felt tears burning the back of her eyes. She fought hard not to let them spill, but they did. "I think you'd better take me home."

Donna dropped Gina off.

"Do you want me to come in?" Donna said.

"No, thanks. I just want to be alone with my thoughts right now."

"Okay. I'll call you soon."

"Thanks, Donna."

Gina went inside, poured herself a glass of wine, and cried. She let all her fear and frustrations out in her sobs. She didn't want to not be with Crockett once the semester ended. She knew she had finals to focus on, but all she wanted to think about was her and Crockett. She stood up, took a deep breath, and headed for bed. She needed to be strong for just a few more weeks.

CHAPTER TWENTY-ONE

Crockett was hurrying through grading all her final papers. She told herself it was so she could get it done and start her vacation, but she knew there was more to it. She needed to get her grades done and sent in so she could contact Gina and see if she was still willing to see her again. She'd been worried ever since that night she'd seen her at the club with Donna. She knew Donna's reputation. But they hadn't been acting like an item, and Donna had even suggested she dance with Gina. So, maybe she had nothing to fear, but she still couldn't shake it.

She read Gina's final story. It was another love story between women, and it was beautiful. She easily gave it an A. She refused to allow herself to analyze the hell out of it as she didn't want to spend that kind of time on it. She finished grading the rest of her Creative Fiction class's work and sent her grades to the Office of the Registrar. Gina was no longer a student of hers.

Crockett had more classes to grade, so she set about doing that. She worked that evening in her office until five o'clock, then packed up her laptop and took it home for more grading over the weekend. She wanted to feel lighthearted, to be sure this meant she'd be back with Gina that night, but she had too many concerns. Maybe she shouldn't approach her. What if Gina didn't want her back? Would she be able to stand the heartache? But she had to try.

She went home, showered, and dressed in some black Dockers with a long-sleeved purple shirt and a black V-neck sweater. She grabbed her jacket on and paced.

"What should I do?" she asked Archie. He simply purred. "A lot of help you are. Should I call or just show up?"

Archie snuggled deeper into the couch and purred louder.

Crockett put her jacket on and grabbed her keys.

"Wish me luck," she told Archie and she was out the door.

She drove to a mini-mart to buy some beer and some wine. She drove by a florist and bought some flowers. She showed up at Gina's and parked in her usual spot. And there she sat. She stared at Gina's door for several minutes. She saw Gina's car was there so knew she was home. She just needed to work up the nerve to knock on the door.

Her beer was getting warm, and if she didn't act soon the flowers would probably start to wilt. She got out of the truck and walked to Gina's door. She took a deep breath and knocked.

Gina answered the door wearing a long brown skirt and a short sweater with a shirt underneath. Crockett thought she'd never looked better. She just stood there, not saying a word.

"Are those for me?" Gina pointed to the flowers.

"Huh? Oh, yeah. Here you go. And I brought you some wine, too."

"Thank you. Come on in."

Crockett walked in and Gina closed the door behind her.

"I bought some beer, too."

"Why don't you put it in the fridge?" Gina followed Crockett into the kitchen. "You seem nervous."

"I guess I am. It's not every day I set myself up for rejection."

"And you really think I'd reject you?"

"I don't know. It was a long semester."

"Did you *read* any of the stories I sent you?" Gina said.

"Of course I did. I graded them, didn't I? But I didn't dare to hope they referred to us."

"Where else would I have gotten the ideas for them?"

"So you're saying you'll take me back?" Crockett said.

"Oh, Crockett. I've waited all these months to take you back. I'd be a fool not to."

"You mean that?"

"I do."

Crockett closed the distance between them and took Gina in her arms. She felt so right there. It was as if no time had passed, like she'd never missed a moment of holding her. She lowered her mouth and brushed her lips against Gina's. The electricity that flowed there made her knees buckle.

"Damn, Gina," Crockett said when she stood straight. "I've missed you."

"I've missed you too."

"Let's go to dinner and dancing. We need to celebrate."

"Wouldn't you rather celebrate here?" Gina said.

Crockett felt her boxers dampen at the thought.

"Well, yeah. That does sound better to me."

Gina took her hand and led her down the hallway. Crockett stood on shaky legs and kissed Gina again. She ran her tongue along Gina's lips and Gina parted hers and welcomed Crockett inside. Their tongues danced together in a tango of lust. Crockett's heart pounded in her chest. Her desire for Gina threatened to consume her.

She unbuttoned Gina's sweater and laid it over the back of the chair. She took her shirt over her head and did the same. She stood staring at Gina's beautiful, voluptuous breasts barely confined by a brown bra. Crockett admired them for only a moment before she unhooked Gina's bra and took her firm breasts in her hands.

Crockett kneaded Gina's breasts and ran her thumbs over her nipples. They responded and Gina moaned. Crockett unzipped Gina's skirt and helped her step out of it. Crockett eased Gina down on the bed and knelt to peel off her panties. She rested her cheek on Gina's inner thigh and inhaled. There was that familiar scent, the one that made blood rush to her brain. She inhaled deeply again before leaning forward to taste her.

She ran her tongue over her and in her before moving her mouth to her slick, swollen clit. She sucked it between her lips and played over it with her tongue. She slid her fingers deep inside her and moved them in and out while she sucked and licked her clit. She felt Gina tightening inside and knew she was close. She kept up her actions and finally Gina clamped around her fingers as she cried out and came again and again.

When Gina's spasms subsided, Crockett slid her fingers out, stood, and undressed. She was sopping wet and was sure evidence of her arousal would run down her leg. She didn't care. She wanted Gina something fierce and didn't care if Gina knew that. She wanted her to. She wanted her to know how hard it had been all those months and how ready she was for her at that moment.

She lay down next to Gina and got even wetter at the feel of the length of Gina's body pressed against hers. Gina rolled over and kissed Crockett hard on the mouth. Crockett kissed her back with a ferocious need. She tried to convey in that kiss how much she craved her touch. Gina must have gotten the message because she skimmed her hand down Crockett's body until it came to rest between her legs.

"Oh my God, you're so wet," Gina said.

"I need you."

"God, I need you, too."

"Please, babe. Don't tease me. Please take care of me."

"Mm."

Gina buried her fingers inside Crockett. She twisted her hand as she withdrew them, then plunged them in again. She repeated this action until Crockett was writhing on the bed with need.

"Please," she said. "Please get me off."

Gina rubbed her thumb over Crockett's clit, and Crockett's world split into a million pieces. Gina continued to rub her and Crockett went into orbit several more times. When she'd finally had enough, she pulled Gina into her arms and held her.

"This is nice," Gina said.

"It is."

"I've missed it so much."

"Me, too."

They dozed for a few minutes and Gina woke to Crockett inside her once again. She moved against her, driving her deeper. She gyrated to make sure all her favorite spots got stroked. She cried out as Crockett took her to one climax after another.

"Damn, I've missed you," Crockett said as she climbed up next to Gina.

"I've missed you, too. And thank you. That was wonderful. Now, your turn."

"No. I'm fine for now. It'll be my turn when we get home. I meant what I said about taking you out for dinner and dancing."

"That would be wonderful," Gina said.

"We'd better take a shower," Crockett said. "I'm sure we reek of sex."

"True."

They took their shower, where Gina rested her forehead on the shower wall while Crockett took her from behind. Gina cried out as Crocket took her to an incredibly powerful orgasm.

"You're amazing," Gina said.

"No. You are."

"We're amazing together," Gina said.

"Yeah, we are."

They toweled each other off and put on their clothes again. All set, Gina stood looking at Crockett.

"What?" Crockett said.

"I just can't believe you're here. I can't believe no one snatched you up. You're here. With me. And I'm the happiest woman in the world."

Crockett took Gina to Basque Norte again. They enjoyed the wine and food and were in a mellow space when they left the restaurant.

"I am so full," Gina said.

"Can you handle dancing?"

"Oh, yeah. The food will settle soon."

"Good. Because now that you're mine again, I want to show you off to the world."

"You're so sweet."

"I can't help it. I just can't believe that damned semester is over and no one decided to make them yours. Not even Donna."

"Donna didn't stand a chance. And she knew it. She knew I wasn't ready to close the door on us."

"I'm glad."

"And you? No women showed any interest?"

"There might have been interested women, but I didn't reciprocate."

"Good. I was worried," Gina said.

"No need. It wouldn't have felt right, you know?"

"I do know. Believe me."

They got to the club and it was packed. They parked in one of the last parking places and went inside. There was no table open so they found a spot at the bar and Gina took a seat while Crockett leaned against it. They sipped their drinks for a while before Gina finally decided she was ready to dance.

"Come on," she said. She took Crockett's hand and led her to the dance floor. She'd forgotten how strong Crockett's hand was. And how right it felt in her own.

They danced for several songs before making their way back to the bar. They were sitting there silently enjoying their drinks and listening to the music when an attractive woman came up and spoke to Crockett.

"Hey, good-lookin'. You want to dance?"

Gina watched Crockett stand up a little straighter.

"Gabby, I'd like you to meet my girlfriend, Gina. Gina, this is Gabby."

Gabby arched an eyebrow.

"Girlfriend. That was quick."

"Not really," Crockett said. "We were together before school started and then she ended up in one of my classes so we were on hold. But the semester is over so we can now date again."

"Well, congratulations, Crockett. I didn't think anyone would ever tie you down. And congrats to you, too, Gina. I wish you both much happiness."

They danced a little more before a slow song came on. Gina watched Crockett open her arms and invite her in. She moved in and wrapped her arms around Crockett's neck. They moved as one with Crockett holding Gina close. When the song ended, Gina looked up to see the desire and something else burning in Crockett's eyes. Crockett bent her head and kissed her. It was brief but said so much, and Gina felt her heart swell.

"Let's get out of here," Gina said.

"Sounds good to me."

Crockett took her hand and led her out to the parking lot. She pressed Gina against her truck and kissed her passionately. Gina's whole body responded to the kiss. She felt it to her toes. She kissed her back with all the emotions she felt for Crockett. She hoped Crockett could feel them.

They got back to Gina's apartment.

"Would you like another beer?" Gina said.

"No, thanks. I just want you."

"That sounds wonderful."

They walked down the hall to Gina's room. They slowly undressed each other until they both stood naked. Gina stepped into Crockett's arms and relished in the feel of Crockett's tight body against hers.

"Lie down," Crockett said. "I need you."

They lay down together and Crockett ran her hand over the length of Gina. Every spot she touched came alive. Gina's whole body tingled as she waited impatiently for Crockett to please her.

Crockett finally slipped her hand between Gina's legs and moved her fingers deep inside her. She plunged them as deep as they would go before pulling them out and doing it again. Gina arched off the bed to meet each thrust. Each one felt deeper than the last. Gina felt Crockett so far inside, she was sure her whole hand must be buried in her.

Crockett moved down Gina's body until she was positioned between her legs. She continued to move her fingers in and out while she took Gina's swollen clit in her mouth. Gina drew in a sharp breath. She was so close; she was sure she would come any minute. And still Crockett worked her magic. Finally, she felt one stroke of Crockett's tongue over her sensitive nerve center and her whole world shattered. One orgasm after another rolled over her and she rode wave after wave.

When she could finally focus again, she realized a needy Crockett was lying right next to her and she hadn't given her any attention. She sucked on one nipple and then another while Crockett squirmed on the bed under her. Gina knew she could make Crockett come that way, but wanted to drag it out, to make her wait. She kissed lower until she was positioned between her legs. Gina buried her tongue deep inside Crockett and savored her flavor. She was delicious and Gina could have stayed there all day pleasing her. She took her time and dragged her tongue all over her.

"Please," Crockett said. "Please, babe. I can't wait any longer. You're making me crazy."

Gina flicked her tongue across Crockett's clit and Crockett screamed as she came over and over again. Gina lay next to Crockett who was running her fingers through Gina's hair.

"Hey, babe? I have a question for you."

Gina propped herself up on an elbow.

"What's up?"

"You know those stories you wrote for class?"

"Sure."

"In them, the characters were in love."

Gina felt butterflies fluttering in the pit of her stomach. What was Crockett getting at? Was she going to tell her she wasn't in love with her? Or that she was? She didn't know if she was ready to have this conversation.

"Yeah."

"So, are we in love?" Crockett said.

Gina thought long and hard. She could lie and keep things casual. Or she could tell the truth and potentially scare Crockett away. She finally opted for the truth.

"I can't speak for you, but I know I am," Gina said.

"I am too, babe. I am too."

About the Author

MJ Williamz was raised on California's central coast, which she left at age seventeen to pursue an education. She graduated from Chico State and it was in Chico that she rediscovered her love of writing. It wasn't until she moved to Portland, however, that her writing really took off, with the publication of her first short story in 2003.

MJ is the author of twelve books, including three Goldie Award winners. She has also had over thirty short stories published, most of them erotica with a few romances and a few horrors thrown in for good measure. She lives in Houston with her wife and fur babies. You can reach her at mjwilliamz@aol.com

Books Available from Bold Strokes Books

Beauty and the Boss by Ali Vali. Ellis Renois is at the top of the fashion world, but she never expects her summer assistant Charlotte Hamner to tear her heart and her business apart like sharp scissors through cheap material. (978-162639-919-8)

Fury's Choice by Brey Willows. When gods walk amongst humans, can two women find a balance between love and faith? (978-1-62639-869-6)

Lessons in Desire by MJ Williamz. Can a summer love stand a four-month hiatus and still burn hot? (978-1-63555-019-1)

Lightning Chasers by Cass Sellars. For Sydney and Parker, being a couple was never what they had planned. Now they have to fight corruption, murder, and enemies hiding in plain sight just to hold on to each other. Lightning Series, Book Two (978-1-62639-965-5)

Summer Fling by Jean Copeland. Still jaded from a breakup years earlier, Kate struggles to trust falling in love again when a summer fling with sexy young singer Jordan rocks her off her feet. (978-1-62639-981-5)

Take Me There by Julie Cannon. Adrienne and Sloan know it would be career suicide to mix business with pleasure, however tempting it is. But what's the harm? They're both consenting adults. Who would know? (978-1-62639-917-4)

The Girl Who Wasn't Dead by Samantha Boyette. A year ago, someone tried to kill Jenny Lewis. Tonight she's ready to find out who it was. (978-1-62639-950-1)

Unchained Memories by Dena Blake. Can a woman give herself completely when she's left a piece of herself behind? (978-1-62639-993-8)

Walking Through Shadows by Sheri Lewis Wohl. All Molly wanted to do was go backpacking…in her own century. (978-1-62639-968-6)

A Lamentation of Swans by Valerie Bronwen. Ariel Montgomery returns to Sea Oats to try to save her broken marriage but soon finds herself also fighting to save her own life and catch a murderer. (978-1-62639-828-3)

Freedom to Love by Ronica Black. What happens when the woman who spent her lifetime worrying about caring for her family, finally finds the freedom to love without borders? (978-1-63555-001-6)

House of Fate by Barbara Ann Wright. Two women must throw off the lives they've known as a guardian and an assassin and save two rival houses before their secrets tear the galaxy apart. (978-1-62639-780-4)

Planning for Love by Erin Dutton. Could true love be the one thing that wedding coordinator Faith McKenna didn't plan for? (978-1-62639-954-9)

Sidebar by Carsen Taite. Judge Camille Avery and her clerk, attorney West Fallon, agree on little except their mutual attraction, but can their relationship and their careers survive a headline-grabbing case? (978-1-62639-752-1)

Sweet Boy and Wild One by T. L. Hayes. When Rachel Cole meets soulful singer Bobby Layton at an open mic, she is immediately in thrall. What she soon discovers will rock her world in ways she never imagined. (978-1-62639-963-1)

To Be Determined by Mardi Alexander and Laurie Eichler. Charlie Dickerson escapes her life in the US to rescue Australian wildlife with Pip Atkins, but can they save each other? (978-1-62639-946-4)

True Colors by Yolanda Wallace. Blogger Robby Rawlins plans to use First Daughter Taylor Crenshaw to get ahead, but she never planned on falling in love with her in the process. (978-1-62639-927-3)

Unexpected by Jenny Frame. When Dale McGuire falls for Rebecca Harper, the mother of the son she never knew she had, will Rebecca's troubled past stop them from making the family they both truly crave? (978-1-62639-942-6)

Canvas for Love by Charlotte Greene. When ghosts from Amelia's past threaten to undermine their relationship, Chloé must navigate the greatest romance of her life without losing sight of who she is. (978-1-62639-944-0)

Heart Stop by Radclyffe. Two women, one with a damaged body, the other a damaged spirit, challenge each other to dare to live again. (978-1-62639-899-3)

Repercussions by Jessica L. Webb. Someone planted information in Edie Black's brain and now they want it back, but with the protection of shy former soldier Skye Kenny, Edie has a chance at life and love. (978-1-62639-925-9)

Spark by Catherine Friend. Jamie's life is turned upside down when her consciousness travels back to 1560 and lands in the body of one of Queen Elizabeth I's ladies-in-waiting…or has she totally lost her grip on reality? (978-1-62639-930-3)

Taking Sides by Kathleen Knowles. When passion and politics collide, can love survive? (978-1-62639-876-4)

Thorns of the Past by Gun Brooke. Former cop Darcy Flynn's heart broke when her career on the force ended in disgrace, but perhaps saving Sabrina Hawk's life will mend it in more ways than one. (978-1-62639-857-3)

You Make Me Tremble by Karis Walsh. Seismologist Casey Radnor comes to the San Juan Islands to study an earthquake but finds her heart shaken by passion when she meets animal rescuer Iris Mallery. (978-1-62639-901-3)

Complications by MJ Williamz. Two women battle for the heart of one. (978-1-62639-769-9)

Crossing the Wide Forever by Missouri Vaun. As Cody Walsh and Lillie Ellis face the perils of the untamed West, they discover that love's uncharted frontier isn't for the weak in spirit or the faint of heart. (978-1-62639-851-1)

Fake It Till You Make It by M. Ullrich. Lies will lead to trouble, but can they lead to love? (978-1-62639-923-5)

Girls Next Door by Sandy Lowe and Stacia Seaman eds.. Best-selling romance authors tell it from the heart—sexy, romantic stories of falling for the girls next door. (978-1-62639-916-7)

Pursuit by Jackie D. The pursuit of the most dangerous terrorist in America will crack the lines of friendship and love, and not everyone will make it out under the weight of duty and service. (978-1-62639-903-7)

Shameless by Brit Ryder. Confident Emery Pearson knows exactly what she's looking for in a no-strings-attached hookup, but can a spontaneous interlude open her heart to more? (978-1-63555-006-1)

The Practitioner by Ronica Black. Sometimes love comes calling whether you're ready for it or not. (978-1-62639-948-8)

Unlikely Match by Fiona Riley. When an ambitious PR exec and her super-rich coding geek-girl client fall in love, they learn that giving something up may be the only way to have everything. (978-1-62639-891-7)

Where Love Leads by Erin McKenzie. A high school counselor and the mom of her new student bond in support of the troubled girl, never expecting deeper feelings to emerge, testing the boundaries of their relationship. (978-1-62639-991-4)

Forsaken Trust by Meredith Doench. When four women are murdered, Agent Luce Hansen must regain trust in her most valuable investigative tool—herself—to catch the killer. (978-1-62639-737-8)

Her Best Friend's Sister by Meghan O'Brien. For fifteen years, Claire Barker has nursed a massive crush on her best friend's older sister. What happens when all her wildest fantasies come true? (978-1-62639-861-0)

Letter of the Law by Carsen Taite. Will federal prosecutor Bianca Cruz take a chance at love with horse breeder Jade Vargas, whose dark family ties threaten everything Bianca has worked to protect—including her child? (978-1-62639-750-7)

New Life by Jan Gayle. Trigena and Karrie are having a baby, but the stress of becoming a mother and the impact on their relationship might be too much for Trigena. (978-1-62639-878-8)

Royal Rebel by Jenny Frame. Charity director Lennox King sees through the party girl image Princess Roza has cultivated, but will Lennox's past indiscretions and Roza's responsibilities make their love impossible? (978-1-62639-893-1)

Unbroken by Donna K. Ford. When Kayla and Jackie, two women with every reason to reject Happy Ever After, fall in love, will they have the courage to overcome their pasts and rewrite their stories? (978-1-62639-921-1)

Where the Light Glows by Dena Blake. Mel Thomas doesn't realize just how unhappy she is in her marriage until she meets Izzy Calabrese. Will she have the courage to overcome her insecurities and follow her heart? (978-1-62639-958-7)